A TRUNK FULL OF ZEROES

A TRUNK FULL OF ZEROES

BY

BRIAN TOWNSLEY

A Trunk Full of Zeroes Copyright © 2023 by Starlite Pulp

This book is a work of fiction. Names, characters, businesses, organizations, places, events and incidents are either the product of the author's imagination or are used fictitiously. Any resemblance to actual persons, living or dead, events, or locales is entirely coincidental.
Trunk was originally published in 2015 by RothCo Press

For information, contact : editor@starlitepulp.com
www.starlitepulp.com
Instagram : @starlite_pulp

Book and Cover design by Starlite Pulp
Cover photograph by the awesome Jens Ochlich
(www.autobahn66.com)

ISBN: 979-8-218-29673-5

endless row of business fronts and offices. He turned right on Wellesley
Ave and continued there some two blocks. He stopped in front of a white
stucco Spanish style house with red brick roof tiles and brown window
frames. He had known this to be his destination, of course, though no
amount of forethought had placed him here. Palm trees lined the street,
each leaning east but going nowhere. Such is their strength and burden.
Sonny looked back at the house and fingered a smoke from his nearly
extinguished pack of Chesterfields and lit the thing without ever looking at
it.

The house looked the same. There was a pile of palm fronds
collected on the front lawn. Shortly after he and his wife found this place,
she remarked that it fit her image of the perfect Los Angeles home. Betty
had been from Idaho, he from Tennessee. He didn't know what her
comment meant but figured if she was happy about it, then that was
enough for him. He probably should have asked what she meant. That
was a complaint she had about him—that he just wasn't interested in what
she thought. Which wasn't true, of course—he just didn't see the purpose
behind a twenty-minute conversation on it. Men and women, he thought,
and shook his head at the impossibility of it all. He liked that behind the
house ran a stream out of the context of what Los Angeles represented. He
liked that he could sit on his back steps and listen to the frogs serenade the
bowl of stars in the darkness or stroll down the slight grade and through

the hole in his fence and pick crayfish out of the water when the mood struck him. It was a plot of untarnished authenticity in a city sorely lacking some. It was also the house he returned home to one evening, drunk and angry, and there found his wife in bed with a negro jazz musician. But that wasn't the kicker. They were dead, a smattering of each of their insides blasted amongst one another on his bedroom wall. Maybe *that* had been the kicker, or maybe it had been this: *he* had been the prime suspect. He still couldn't decide, though he wanted nothing more than his wife back. That night back. Better yet, the night before that, to somehow fix what had unbeknownst to him gone awry, like falling asleep in a film and waking only for the climax.

A car honked behind him and he flinched like a librarian and drove off.

2.

Sonny parked in the loading zone in front of the Elmwood Arms Hotel on Grand St in downtown and hustled into the lobby. The coat of arms above the double doors had a shield with a red eagle on it and was missing one of the rusted swords that crossed behind it. The place felt like half the lights were out but Sonny figured it always seemed that way. Easier to conceal the decades of dirt and abuse. The carpet had once been grand but was now threadbare and filthridden though its busy design concealed it nearly as well as the darkness. It was a deep maroon in the corners and less trafficked areas though the walkways were blackened. Matted stains of gum like a negative of stars in the night sky. There was a cigar counter in the corner and Sonny smiled at the blonde manning it. She blew a bubble at him. Her act was disinterest and it was a bad one. Grammar school plays had better performances. He figured he knew where half of the gum stains came from.

The man at the front desk wore a grey suit with maroon epaulets and pocket fringes. He did not smile or allow any movement that might pass for acknowledgement as Sonny approached. As if a universe of activity lay just beyond the emptiness that required his present attention. He was shuffling some papers and looking down at the counter though the lobby was otherwise vacant. Sonny waited. The man still did not react and so Sonny clapped his hand on the service bell loudly three times though the man he sought stood no more than five feet away. The concierge visibly jerked in his agitation and softly placed his uncalloused hand over Sonny's. Finally he smiled.

"May I help you?" He asked with a grin, as if he had not seen Sonny prior.

"You're rude. But that's fine. Lucky for you, I don't need a friendly bellhop," Sonny said, and leveled a gaze not without a hint of malice.

"Sir, I am not a—"

"Bellhop, concierge, manager, circus clown, whatever. You're king of the hill. I need a fucking room. Please."

The man looked like he had just been forced to hold his hand to a hot stove.

"You a little light in the loafers, son?" Sonny asked.

"I beg your pardon, sir. I am not used to being treated in this fashion." His voice was a squeak.

"*Really?* In here?" Sonny took a step back and looked around to see if he had missed anything the first time. "Alright," he continued, "look. Sorry if I offended. I'm just an asshole."

The man looked about to cry.

"*Christ.* Get me a room," Sonny said. "One week. Even if I'm not here that long, I'll pay for it. You keep the rest. Okay?"

"It doesn't really work that way, sir." The man was shaking his head and would not make eye contact now.

"It does for me." Sonny reached into the inside pocket of his coat and pulled out five twenty-dollar bills so crisp they looked brittle. He placed them on the counter.

The hurt expression the man had been wearing like a dress disappeared and he smiled, briefly. He still didn't look at Sonny, instead eyeing the bills as if they might grow legs and clatter away atop the faux marble.

"That cover it?"

"We've got a wonderful penthouse available—"

"I'm sure it's friggin grand. Gimme the key."

"Well, sir, there is paperwork that must be completed first." The clerk looked embarrassed at this admission.

"Sure there is," Sonny admitted. "Give it to me with the key. I'll fill it out and drop it off later."

The clerk looked at him without any given expression.

Sonny gathered the money in his right hand and began to bring it back into his coat.

"That won't be necessary, sir." The man turned and unhooked the key from the board holding nothing but keys.

He handed it over the counter and greedily eyed Sonny's right hand.

"Better make it two of those. There is a woman, actually, a *girl*," he amended, "who might be staying with me."

The clerk smiled then. "*Of course* there will be," he said.

Sonny stared at the man, then leaned over the counter and hissed: "She's a *girl*. She's a friend of mine, like a daughter. Get it? Use that tone of voice with me again."

He remained leaning over the counter.

After some seconds, the concierge asked: "Sir?"

"I mean it. Use that tone of voice again. That smirk."

"Sir, I meant nothing by it." He was looking at the counter again.

"It's all you have. And you meant *everything* by it. Smirk at me again and I'll cut your asshole so big you'll be shitting into a colostomy bag the rest of your life. Get me?" He smiled.

The clerk did not respond. Nobody has ever not responded more.

Sonny leaned back and looked around the lobby. Still empty. Then over at the cigar counter girl, her blonde ringlets and snapping gum. She was reading a magazine, or at least looked that way.

"How you doin down there, toots?"

"Me and my ass are just fine the way they are, thank you," she shouted back, and popped her gum. Her accent was pure Brooklyn. Or fake Brooklyn. Sonny couldn't tell. Too many years in Mexico.

"My two keys, please," he said.

The concierge handed Sonny the second key and tried in vain to keep his hands from shaking.

***

The elevator operator had to be called from the garage as he was pulling double duty in an effort to save the bottom line. It's difficult affording a business with no customers. He was just a boy, and looked to Sonny like the quarterback of a high school football team in Ohio, or Michigan. Some place in the middle. What they refer to as the Midwest which actually is mostly north and not west at all. All-American as Wisconsin cheese. He smiled at Sonny when he first saw him and apologized for being in the garage. Sonny saw nothing to apologize for but nodded to be agreeable. When the boy had closed the gate and door and pulled the requisite lever, he looked again at the sparrows sprouting from either collar on Sonny's tanned neck and pretended not to. The elevator sprang into motion as smoothly as a car wreck.

"Smooth ride, eh?"

"Yessir," the boy said.

"It was a joke."

"Yessir. Eighth floor. Got the penthouse, huh, sir?"

"That's what I hear."

"Well. It's the best." He nodded in confirmation to this fact. "Not many people stay in that room," he said. "Sometimes we get newlyweds. Not for a while though. It's the best." He nodded again.

"Is there such a thing, here?" Sonny asked, without sarcasm.

The boy looked at him and said nothing. Finally: "Are you from LA, sir?"

"Is anyone?"

"I'm not. I just moved out here from Iowa. I'm gonna be an actor. My parents said I could do it. I think I can." He paused. Waited for a response. Upon failing to receive one, he continued: "Haven't had any callbacks yet." He snapped his fingers and clapped his hands in the rhythm of habit, and continued: "I know I gotta pay my dues though." He smiled then. It was a great smile.

"Acting's not an easy gig," Sonny said in reply, and tried to keep himself from smirking disdainfully.

"I'm sure I can do it though."

Sonny looked at the boy and wondered if ever he himself had been so idealistic about anything. So naïve. He doubted it. Even back when life had certain rules and routines he understood and chose to follow. Even then.

Sonny grinned back at the grinning boy and looked at the passing of lighted floors. He had counted to eight many times in his life but none seemed to suspend time the way this trip did.

"Does every elevator trip take this long, or am I just getting a luxury ride because of the penthouse?"

"Yessir. This isn't really the quickest elevator, is it?"

"Empires have fallen in a shorter time, son."

"Yessir."

"What's your name? I thought you guys carried nametags."

"Charles, sir."

"Do people call you Chuck?"

"No sir," he turned and smiled.

"Too young for a Chuck. Well, Chuck, I'll be here for a week, give or take. And being that we're bound to spend the rest of our lives together in this elevator—"

"We'll be there soon, sir."

"Don't defend the elevator, son. You didn't build the damn thing."

"Yessir."

The elevator stopped. They both looked up at the lighted number 8 in disbelief. Chuck opened the gate and bent to pick up Sonny's bag but Sonny beat him to it.

"I'm Sonny, by the way."

"Nice to meet you, Sonny. Sir."

Sonny smiled and twirled the keys on his finger and turned to the hallway. He heard the gate close behind him and eventually the car lurched downward. Someday it may reach the bottom, Sonny thought.

The room was a suite with a living area and a bedroom and a stamp-sized bathroom. There were yellows and blues and tans and it was all offensive in its attempt at being inoffensive. He dropped his bag on the couch. He walked the place once and turned on the radio to a whisper. *Sentimental Me* was playing and Sonny walked out on the small concrete deck. He grabbed the blueglass ashtray from the table and put it on the railing and lit a Chesterfield. Below, the city moved in seams, the inching of cars scurrying on concrete. He had missed this place. Upon leaving Los Angeles he had no idea he would long for any part of the landscape here. His wife, sure. He exhaled into the windy day, the smoke physically evident and then not. Once inside, he closed the blackout blinds in an artificial night and lay down on the bed in his clothes. Newborns should

sleep so well.

3.

Sonny awoke that evening in a womb of blackness. A single pinstripe of light ran between the crease of the curtains and eventually he made sense of the room. The clock next to the bed said it was 8:18 p.m.

He showered. Shaved. Pomaded his hair and hatted himself. He was outfitted in a white collared shirt and flatfront trousers, brogues, and his snapcap. His undershirt could be seen through his collared shirt. He stared at the jacket that lay on his bed in indecision. Nobody needs a jacket in LA, he thought. Finally, he reached into his bag and pulled out the semi-auto in the side pocket and dropped it into his jacket pocket and draped the thing over his forearm. He looked at himself in the mirror, inspected his shaving job, and left for The Union Jack. To check in on Katie.

He took one look at the elevator and turned toward the stairwell.

***

He drove with the windows open to the night air and smoked a cigarette for vitality. At least that's what the billboard he passed had said. What would she be now? 16? Jesus, 16, he thought. And Emma?

The Union Jack was a lounge on Sunset Boulevard run by a one-eyed Brit whom Sonny had worked out of a jam some years back. He hoped the place was still there. He was putting a lot of faith in the hopes of a joint he hadn't seen in four years. But there it was—said flag waving above the black entrance door. No windows. There was parking in the rear besides the street in front and he pulled the mercury into the alley and cut the engine. Left his coat sprawled atop the backseat like a drunkard. He walked to the back door of the Union Jack and knocked thrice, slowly and in rhythm, then twice more, quickly. He had no idea if the same code was still used but saw no reason not to try. The door was pulled back and there in the doorway was a lean mulatto man chewing on a toothpick disinterestedly with a gun in his waistband. His eyelids drooped so low that he looked either half-awake or fully under the influence, though Sonny knew differently. The man was wearing a brown fedora, long-brimmed with a teardrop crown, crushed low on his head and a white shirt with brown suspenders. He looked at Sonny without recollection.

"Can I 'elp ya?"

"Ray."

"I know you, mate?"

He looked Sonny over again, his left hand inching near his belt. Sonny had once seen Ray stack a man much larger than himself with a single blow on the surprise account of his being a lefty and the hook that hid behind it.

"Sonny Haynes," Sonny said in a whisper, as way of reintroduction.

"'Oly shit! My apologies, man!"

He looked yet again at Sonny, then stepped forward and slapped him on the shoulder in greeting.

"Been inked up a bit then?" he said, and made a doodle with his finger as if following the ink about. "I heard you might'a gone down bloody Mexico way? Ya still got that warrant on ya shoulder, then?"

Sonny smiled and said nothing. Then: "There a game goin' tonight?"

"'Course, mate. Ya lookin to buy in?"

"Naw. Looking for one of the players. You know," he said, and smiled at Ray and his twirling toothpick. "Mick here?"

"He's up front. You lookin for Katie, yah? She's in there robbin them blokes blind. As always." He smiled and shook his head. "Hey, bloody good to see you, ya bastid," he said.

They shook hands and Ray moved aside to allow Sonny passage down the dark hall. He passed two restroom doors on his left and one door painted black on his right that he would enter before long. He passed them all and instead slid through the curtain of beads that led to the lounge.

The room was jarring not because of the change from the black hallway he had left behind but because of the redness that it contained. It was like drowning in a swirling riptide of red and closing your red eyelids while pondering the philosophical underpinnings of red. Red like that. The mahogany bar stretched along most of the eastern wall and below it sat twelve stools with red vinyl seats and brass nailheads. The rest of the room was a cacophony of brown wood and red vinyl—tables, booths, chairs. Lights designed to look like red candles squatted in the middle of each table and the lights that hung above carried red fixtures. The walls hung pictures of foxhunts with men in red coats and black hats directing their steeds above a cluster of spotted hounds. All pendant. And behind the bar hung a massive British flag of fine stitching, torn and frayed at the ends and holed in places.

Sonny walked to the bar and the bartender there conversing with a couple who sat on stools. The place was mostly full tonight of brillantined men and bobby-pinned women and no one yet had looked Sonny's way. A single sat in each red corner, lonely as lighthouses. He leaned on the northernmost stool and waited. Finally, the heavyset man behind the bar with long gray hair and an eye patch lumbered toward him and asked: "What's yer poison, man?"

"Manhattan. Rocks."

The man looked down to the floor and said nothing.

Finally he spoke: "Now, the proper way to serve the Manhattan is chilled without ice, lad. But I'll"—and upon connecting the voice to the face—"*well I'll be swallowed whole and shat out the ass of a Mexican!*"

He barreled towards Sonny and reached across the bar violently and pulled Sonny's face to his chest. He placed hands like porterhouses on either side of Sonny's cheeks and brought him face to face.

"What kept ya so? Ya fucking bastard!"

"All them Mexican women," Sonny said, and smiled.

The big man reared back and laughed fit to kill himself, a bellow that Sonny felt certain had alarmed any wild animals in the nearby hills.

"Ya come to kill 'em all, Sonny?"

"I just came home is all, Mick," Sonny said.

Sonny lit a cigarette and stared at Mick who was staring at him.

"Ya just came home is all? Is that right? Just came home like Odysseus, disguised in rags and without thought of revenge? Well, we're damn happy to have ya." His smile did no justice to the words.

He began to make the Manhattan.

"I don't need that, Mick," and put his hand out in confirmation. "Been off the juice for a while." He sighed at the thought of it. "Make me a pot of coffee, would ya?"

Mick squinted at him through one eye and laughed.

"All that desert air down there make ya smarter? Ya should have been off this stuff years ago, way ya act on it. Coffee it is. What's with all the artwork?" He motioned about sonny's arms and neck.

"I'm gonna head back to the room. See Emma and Katie."

"I'll bring the coffee back, Son. But ya won't find Emma."

But Sonny had turned and swam through the beads once again and into the black hallway and there the door on his left. He stared at it before opening it though there was nothing to see but what the mind conjures upon finding no image to grasp at all.

There was a lock on the door impossible to see in the given light. It was bolted into the ground and moved easily enough in the darkness by the knowing and not at all by those without. He slid the springbolt up in silence and turned the knob and entered the room.

There was a circular table underneath the haloed and soft light and the red felt on the table shone like velvet. There were five players tonight, four men and one teenage girl. Each of them had already lost multiple hands to the girl but would deny it to a man upon first light.

Of the current hand, two of the men had folded and sat with their arms bent on the table pondering ways out of the present. Katie with her back to Sonny. Her two opponents sat across the table. One wore his hat so low you could barely see the tip of his formidable nose. The other was hatless and wore a burnt orange plaid sportcoat of the sort that had never once been in style. To this day. His hair shone like steel. The hatted player threw two chips into the piled collection centered on the table and called.

The cards were laid down like they were breakable.

Sonny couldn't see the specifics but Katie rose in her chair and pulled the pile of red and white plastic towards her. She had grown. She began to stack her booty atop her given piles when the burnt orange man muttered, "Not normal for one player to have that much luck." As if it were the old west. As if it were a western film. The other players said nothing. Finally the hatted man without a face nodded towards Sonny and said, "You gettin in the game or are ya here to get us drinks?"

The other men laughed at this.

Katie turned then, looked once and immediately again like her head was on a swivel. She said nothing but was immediately up and with a single step and a bounce into Sonny's arms, all hundred pounds of her draped from his neck like a family locket.

She was sixteen now, but Sonny had seen enough in that one step to realize where she had grown. She had a woman's breasts and the tightness of youth. Her black sweater hugged her frame like it enjoyed the task. He found himself spinning her in his arms not so much out of gaiety but for fear the men at the table may witness more of her than was acceptable. When he had left, she had been 12. Just a girl, he thought.

She pulled away from him and looked at him and wiped once with her thumb at the inked tear and locked eyes with him. "I knew you'd come back for me," she said. "I knew it. *I've waited for this*," she said into his ear.

Her eyes were large for her face and the shards of green in the brown pupils shone in the dim light. She had a thin line of freckles that ran the course of her nose and peppered each cheek. Her father had been Hawaiian and had given her that milky brown tone, the only thing of worth he had passed down. Sonny wiped her bobbed hair out of her eyes and then looked at the table and the leering there. She was running her hands over him like he was a new toy and it was shamefully comfortable. He grabbed her hands and held them like setting them in handcuffs and smiled.

"Where's your mom?" he asked.

She looked at him and then back at the table and said nothing.

"Is she around tonight?" Sonny continued.

Katie turned her head towards the table, then the rest of her.

"It seems my night has ended before I end all of yours, boys," Katie addressed the table, smiling.

Such talk was barely tolerable from any winner but never from a girl. One of the men who had folded the previous hand said "You're gonna just shove off without even givin us a chance to get our money back?"

"Another night, gentlemen. Act like you got a set," Sonny answered.

There was a general murmur of discontent at the table. The hatted man pushed his chair back as if to stand.

"You're not takin the girl without her playin more hands," he said. It sounded like an ultimatum.

Katie broke free of Sonny and stepped quickly to the table and deposited the chips into a bag that lay in shadow next to her chair. As she did that Sonny stepped towards the hatted man.

"I appreciate you settin an agenda for my night," Sonny said.

"It aint got nothin to do with you, friend. But she aint leavin. Not yet."

Sonny panned the table and all eyes on him. None stood.

"Look pal, this is our money," faceless said. "Our *rent*."

"Then ya shouldn'ta bet it, dumbass," Sonny said, and smiled at the thought that he would have said the same thing when he was a cop, a million years ago.

"Awww, come on fella," one of the men at the table said. Sonny didn't look down to see who.

"Didn't you guys *realize* two hands into this thing that she could take the lot of you and carry on a telephone conversation at the same time?" Sonny asked, clearly exasperated with their incompetence.

"It's a *FIX!*," the hatted man said.

He stood and pointed past Sonny at Katie and as he did Sonny grabbed that hand and pulled it towards him and lowered it. He brought his knee up violently and forced it into and through the underside of the man's elbow. The snap echoed in the silence and would remind everyone in the room later of the break in a pool game. Simple physics really. With his left hand he pulled the man's hat even lower so that it covered his face entire and he used the given momentum to kick the man into a dark corner. There the man scuffed into the darkness and sat on his knees screaming but no one was really paying attention. All eyes were on the thick tattooed man who had just entered their lives and would now be leaving. Sonny looked each man down and grabbed the screamer in the corner and rushed him out of the room and into the hallway and out the back door into the alley. Immediately he burst back into the room and Katie had her hand extended and she in a giddy laughter then and he tipped his hat to the table and the two of them exited the room, his hand cradling hers as they stepped almost in unison in some bastardized tango of the absurd.

As they exited the room, Mick was walking through the beaded doorway with a mug of coffee. He was but a silhouette, though a stout-barreled one at that.

"Ya causin' bloody trouble already?" he asked, with a hint of mirth.

"Shit. Yeah. Maybe. Look, sorry, Mick."

Sonny reached out and took the coffee with his free hand.

Mick looked at Katie and said, "He returned. He came back for you and your mum, like ya said he would."

"I *told* you he would," she said to him, and nodded towards the bag in her hand. "Got some chips to cash in here."

"You'll take care of 'er, then?" Mick said, looking at Sonny.

"Like she was mine," Sonny said, and kissed the girl on her forehead.

"She *is* now," the big man said, without explanation. He nodded at Katie and took the bag of chips from her hand. "What's all that hollerin outside? That your work?" He asked.

Sonny nodded in the darkness, still confused by the big man's confession.

4.

The four of them—Sonny, Katie, Ray, Mick—kneeled around the man in the alley like he was a ball and they in preparation for a rugby scrum. Sonny sipped his steaming coffee. The wounded man was holding the broken arm by the bicep and looking up at the faces intermittently and between sobs and grunts would say "Asshole!" or "Fuck!" towards the collected faces and then return to his singular pain.

Finally it was Mick who spoke: "Looks like ya got a broken elbow, then. How did ya go about gettin that?"

"How the hell do you think? From that—," he spit then, inarticulately and half-drool, and continued: "That asshole with the tattoos! I didn't do nothin to him! God dammit this *hurts*!" He grimaced again at the pavement.

"I'd be watchin me bloody gob bout now, mate," Ray said, as way of advice.

"*Fuck you*!" The man screamed.

Sonny tossed a bit of the steaming coffee into the man's face then. The brim of the man's hat caught the trim of it while the rest spotted the man's chin and neck. He screamed a pitch higher than anything he had thus far accomplished.

Sonny placed his mug of coffee on the ground and picked the man up with two hands and pressed him against the alley wall and squeezed his jaw in his right hand. Sonny brought his own face mere inches from the hatted one.

"Shut up. Listen to me. *Quit acting.*"

The man tried to speak but could barely move his jaw and so what came out of his mouth sounded like he was gargling.

"I broke your arm clean. You'll be *fine.* I'll even drive ya to the damn hospital. But shut the hell up and quit embarrassing yourself in front of a woman. *Girl,*" he amended.

They both looked then at Katie who looked back at them with tambourine eyes that consciously blinked on cue like a doe's.

Mick and Ray looked at each other and Ray walked back inside the club.

Mick patted Sonny on the shoulder and whispered something in his ear. Then he smiled at the onearmed man and said, "Now I *know* you know better than to use my establishment in any conversations you might be havin' at the hospital." He slapped the man then, hard but playfully, across the cheek, and winked at Katie with his one eye in the dark alley and

was gone.

"Now here's the deal, fella," Sonny said. "You climb in my back

seat and I'll drive ya to the hospital. Complain one time and I'll drop ya

where I stop. Get it?"

The fella nodded.

Sonny let go of the man's chin then, and his hand had gripped it

solidly enough to provide a thin amorphous bruise that would last the

better part of a week. The man removed his hat, and still holding his right

bicep, entered the back seat upon the door being opened for him. He sat

there and looked up at Sonny through the back window like any perp that

he had collected over the years. Inconsequential and false.

"Oh, hand me that jacket," Sonny said. "It's got my gun in it, and

I'd hate for it to fall into the wrong hands."

The man looked at the jacket splayed across the seat and a moment

passed when the small thoughts of each affected the future entire. Then

the man slowly cradled the jacket in his one arm and passed it to Sonny.

"Good boy," Sonny said.

Sonny drove the night streets like he owned them. The Mercury slid about

the concrete like a predator, full of a stealthy bravado. They headed east to

Fountain Avenue and there Cedars of Lebanon Hospital. He stopped the car and reached his arm across the backrests of the front seats and looked at the man. EMERGENCY wore red letters that blinked in the spring night.

"Here we are. That'll be ten dollars," Sonny said.

"I-I don't have..."

"I'm kidding, of course." He smiled.

The man in back said nothing. His eyes told story enough that he was done with the night though truth be told it was only beginning.

"You went to a bar on Sunset. You were walking to your car in the alley when a guy jumped you and—gimme your wallet."

"What?"

"*Gimme your friggin wallet* or I'll drop ya off in the middle of Darktown with no pants and a broken arm. *Christ.*"

Katie laughed from the front seat and turned up the radio. Billie Holliday was singing *Night and Day* like the moon's radiance depended on it.

The man handed Sonny his wallet. He proceeded to take all the cash out and handed it to Katie.

"They won't believe the mugging story if you've still got cash. Eight bucks. Whooo. High roller coming through. Gimme the rest."

The man looked at him with wide eyes intended to display disbelief.

"I know damn well you didn't walk into the game with the buy-in plus eight bucks. And if you did, and your intention was to stiff the little lady here, then I aint lettin you outta the car anyway," Sonny said.

He leveled a look at the man and said: "Pony up."

The man began to reach down to his sock and Sonny punched the man then with a short, violent backhanded right that splintered the man's nose instantly, the wet sound of which resonated in the car like an exclamation point without a sentence to accompany it. The man began bleeding instantly and looked at Sonny then like he missed his mother, saying nothing intelligible. Sonny, for his part, handed the man a white handkerchief. "Anything else comes up from that sock besides cash and you won't have time to use it," Sonny said, and in his left hand draped the .45 over the seat.

The man in the back of the car had never felt so tired. His face throbbed as he gingerly held the handkerchief to his nostrils. He looked down at his sock as if it were a divide unreachable. Then he began the journey, lifting his pant leg and there a pocket swollen with bills. He handed the wad to Sonny, who flipped it to Katie.

"Good soldier. So anyway," Sonny went on as if nothing had happened, "you got jumped and he broke your arm. And now your nose. Or *she* broke 'em, if you're feeling adventurous, and then took the cash from your wallet. Make up whatever amount you'd like to have. Then a kind citizen found you and dropped you off here. The kind citizen is John Doe with brown hair in a Ford and a white shirt. You're kinda banged up, so you wasn't focused on the particulars. You got me?"

The man said nothing but simply nodded, once.

"Good. And you mention me, or my appearance, or this little girl here, or the Union Jack for that matter, and I put it on my wife's grave that I will paint the walls with you." He looked at the man's driver's license in his wallet, and continued: "Jack Margerete of 12333 Doheny Ave. Don't make me visit. I don't go to that side of town much anyway." He tucked the license into his shirt pocket.

The man nodded again and accepted the emptied wallet as it was given him. He struggled out of the car there and slouched his way towards the ER, his hat askew, one arm clung to the mangled bicep of the other. Broke. Broken.

5.

They sat at Pink's eating hot dogs. Sonny added extra mustard and sauerkraut and Katie ate hers plain. That had never changed. Even in 1941, nine years ago, when Sonny would finish his shift and pick Emma and Katie up at some ungodly hour of night, it was Pink's, plain. The consistency of repetition. He wished he could say the same for the rest of her. For the rest of all of them.

Sonny counted seven the amount of men that had craned their necks to look at her as they waited in line along La Brea. This was gonna be harder than he had imagined, he thought. Finally seeing her across the table, he was okay with it being harder though.

"So, you seen Harold?" Sonny asked.

"Nope. Not in a couple years," she said. "He checked in a couple of times. You asked him to, right?"

Sonny nodded as he chewed his hot dog.

"Yeah. Well, you know." She waved her hand dismissively and with her eyes did something at once youthful and wearied. Then she added: "His wife left him, you know..."

"Celeste? She left him?"

"Yeah. But I don't know much about it. Mom told me—you know how she always knew everything before anyone else."

"Well. It's hard. Being married to a cop, I mean." He winked at her. "Hey," he said, "I brought something back for you."

She grinned like a little girl and Sonny felt everything weaken at once.

"I brought it back from Mexico. Got it from this carnival I visited." He pulled out a leather string with a small skeleton hanging pendant. "It's from, uhh, el dia de la muerte—the day of the dead. Down there they celebrate—"

"Yeah. I know about it," she said. Her smile could have lit Gilmore Field. "I love it." She took it from his hand and held it up to the light as if it were a precious stone. "Will you put it on?" She asked him.

Sonny stood and walked behind her and set into place the fragile clasp. He had to keep from staring at her neck as he did so.

The skeleton hung from between her collarbones like a gallows for the blessed.

Sonny sat again and said: "It's...uh. I hope you like it."

"It's perfect. I won't ever take it off," Katie said, and continued smiling into the night. She looked at him with adoration. He looked away.

"So you been cleared of Betty's murder now, right?" She asked.

Sonny continued looking at anything specific in the room besides her and said nothing.

"You mean—"

She stopped as abruptly as she had begun. She held the remainder of her hot dog pendant in her right hand and her eyes were saucers wide with disbelief.

"I haven't been back here in four years, kiddo. I haven't checked up. Haven't written. Haven't hardly even checked the news but a few times. But I aint hangin around long enough to find out, tell you that." He sipped his soda.

Katie nodded, acutely aware of the situation despite her years. Then she asked: "So where we goin, then?"

" *Whoooaaaa*," Sonny put his hand out in a gesture of stopping and laughed as he chewed.

"What? You don't want me tagging along?"

"Speaking of that, where's your *mom*? She should be here."

Katie's smile disappeared in a fashion that questioned its existence at all. She looked down at the table. She said: "Mom's gone, Sonny."

"Whaddya mean *gone*? Like she's not in L.A.?"

"Gone like she was a prossy and hasn't been around for two years. Gone like she went on a date with a john and never came home." She said it slowly like it were rehearsed and shook her head once at the thought of it. "He was a new guy," she added.

Sonny said nothing. There were too many thoughts in his head at that time for any one to find articulation and thus he stared at her like a math problem unsolvable.

"She's gone. I mean, they never found her—"

It was then that Sonny noticed the rim of tears like hammocks in her eyes and knew that she was continuing only because he wasn't speaking. He moved from his chair in an instant and kneeled next to hers and said: "I'm so sorry. Fuck, I'm sorry." He held her then and it was not awkward or prurient in nature. He was a caretaker and father figure and had known her since she was in grade school. His wife and he had babysat her when her mother came home late or not at all. She was family.

They left Pink's then and walked to the black Mercury in the back parking lot and drove the city down.

***

The story she told brought with it a reality that the night had thus far escaped. Emma had gone on a date with a man named Hank and didn't return. Katie was not alarmed because that happened sometimes. She slept in the hotel room they had been staying in and waited. Played solitaire. Listened to the radio. After two days had passed she called Mick. He picked her up and called the cops. Missing hookers were a high priority like Mickey Cohen was a legitimate businessman.

Emma disappeared less than a year after the Black Dahlia case that would hold Los Angeles is its sway for some fifty years. Emma was never found. No body, no memory. Life moved on.

Katie had stayed with Mick for the last two years. She said she no longer went to school but read books on her own and played poker nearly every night. At Mick's, she hustled the place, taking in whatever the suckers offered up. In some of the other games she played (Mick would call beforehand to vouch for her and get her in), she played conservatively, learning the politics of men. A few times Mick sent Ray with her. She would win as often as she felt it was safe. When it wasn't, she folded like an accordion in a polka band.

Once, she told Sonny, she misjudged the man working the room. He wore a mustache tightly curled at the tips and a grey pinstripe suit. He slicked his hair like Gable and was as gentlemanly as a butler. Katie raked it in. After the last hand, he had smiled at her warmly like a father and took her hand and led her into a hallway behind one of the lounges. He asked for his money back. Katie just stared at him. He smacked her twice and asked again. She told him that he played poker like a 15-year old girl. He beat her so thoroughly that she stayed three nights in the hospital. She remembered the ceiling of the hallway best. White stucco with yellow swirls painted into it, one running into another. She stared at them as he continued to beat her. Until she passed out. There was an attempted rape, but she didn't remember that. She had to be told, at the hospital. It hadn't been "seen through to fruition," as the doctor put it.

By that time Ray had already paid the man a visit, so she was unable to ask him why he hadn't finished the job.

She meandered back to the topic of her mother. Of how much she missed her. Of how she knew she wasn't ever coming back. Of how she had known it less than a week after she had disappeared.

Sonny nodded in confirmation of this. Emma had been many things, but despite her given profession, an irresponsible mother she was not. Their relationship had always seemed more of friends than mother-daughter, but that still left them at best friends. She doted on Katie and would help her with her homework or call Sonny at the slightest worry.

Though neither of them had said it, it was as clear as a running spring that Emma had bought the big ticket and would not be returning from her trip.

Katie had fallen asleep as Sonny cruised the PCH and fed her lies about his time in Mexico. He was grateful that he could stop having to make things up. He was running out of stories that hadn't happened. He felt that he was not good at it. He smoked cigarettes down and followed the moon's reflection on the Pacific.

It was nearly 4 o' clock in the morning when Sonny pulled into the parking lot of the Elmwood Arms. He donned his jacket and picked Katie up in his arms and carried her into the hotel. The man who was working there was named Arnie, according to his nametag. He was seventy if he was a day. His snoring resembled a rhythmic howitzer as Sonny neared the front desk.

Eventually, they reached his room. He lay Katie on the bed as if she were made of glass and tucked her under. He walked to the couch and covered himself in his jacket and slept, his feet hanging off the edge of the thing like he was Gulliver lost in the land of the Lilliputians.

6.

Sonny woke to a false night. He dreamt of green fields and rolling hills of yellow gardenias like he had not seen since a child in Tennessee.

He rived the drapes and took in the city below. It bustled as if it existed without him. Katie was sound asleep on the bed. He found some stationary in the drawer in the end table and set about writing a note:

Katie-

Hope you slept well, sweetie. I am off to take care of some business. Be back later. I'll check in with you.

Sonny

He left the note along with a five-dollar bill on the pillow opposite hers.

He did not bother to shower or shave or even change the clothes he had worn the night before, but rather took the day as an extension of last night. Chuck stood next to him in the elevator and stared at the ceiling.

"You alright there, Chuck?"

"Yessir. You look tired today is all, sir."

"I'm never tired," Sonny said, and smiled at the ridiculousness of the façade.

"Okay."

"Chuck?" Sonny asked.

"Yessir."

"How old are you?"

"I'm 19, sir."

"Jesus Christ. Ninefuckinteen."

"Ummm. Uh-huh."

"I'm 42. Do I look 42?" He rubbed his stubbled chin as he said it as if that might wipe away some years of wear.

"Well, sir. I don't—know how to answer that."

"Jesus Christ. This isn't a fuckin audition, and I'm not a woman. Do I look 42?"

Chuck glanced at Sonny once over and took careful note of the rakish stubble, the crow's feet that spread like roots from the corner of deepset eyes, the speckled graying at the temples. Then he looked back at the ceiling.

"More or less, sir," he finally answered.

"Well, shit," Sonny chuckled. "I prefer less"

"Yessir."

They both looked up at the spectrum of numbers above them like they were things wholly unattainable. They were nearly to the third floor.

"I'm 42 years old. Be careful." He paused to concentrate on the seemingly stagnant elevator. Then: "The next 23 years are pretty fuckin important to you, yeah? Or else you could end up like me."

"Is that a bad thing, Mr...Sonny?" He asked, realizing that he still didn't know Sonny's last name.

Sonny said nothing for a time. The question required some thinking, apparently. Finally, he answered: "I'm vertical, Chuck. I couldn't tell ya why. I've been dead more times than you got fingers, but I'm still vertical. That's gotta count for something." Sonny blushed as the truth felt wholly unfamiliar to him as quantum mathematics.

Chuck smiled at him then. An all-American smile. From Ohio. A quarterback smile.

"You play quarterback in high school, son?," Sonny asked.

"Yessir. All-state."

Sonny patted the boy on the shoulder. "You're gonna do fine in Hollywood," he said. "Play the jock. Tell your agent to look for the trust fund or ivy league roles. You'll be a star, kid."

The elevator doors eventually opened. Nothing was said and nothing else needed to be said. As Sonny walked through the lobby, the flamboyant clerk looked his way and Sonny smiled at him like he was a meal.

Before he reached the door Sonny heard a voice calling to him. It was not a voice he recognized, but was nonetheless the voice of a man who believed he should be telling others what to do but not how to do it, and Sonny knew as much before he ever placed it.

"SIR!," the voice said.

Sonny turned slowly. There was a short man who seemed wider than he was tall standing in the doorway of a room left of the front desk. Sonny knew automatically that he must be the house dick. He was surprised the Elmwood Arms could afford one, and irritated with himself that he hadn't noticed the office the night prior.

"Yes," he answered, and looked around the empty lobby in mock surprise, "I suspect you're referring to me."

"I was wonderin if I might have a word with you," the man said. The accent was all piney woods southern, but exaggerated like in a movie.

"How about right here?"

"How about in my office?" The man asked.

Sonny smiled and walked the lobby again. The man at the front desk was enjoying the scene. The fat man disappeared in the room and Sonny followed him in. It was a room like so many others he had been in throughout his law enforcement career. Utilitarian and completely bereft of any personality whatever. As if the very idea of it might disappoint those faceless and in charge. There was a desk and a chair. Two more chairs opposite. A typewriter. A bulletin board with some papers about policy. More papers on the desk. A coatrack in the corner, coatless.

The man was sitting behind his desk when Sonny entered. His hat was pushed back on his head and he was sweating and breathing heavily. Sonny suspected the sitting had done that. Very taxing, sitting down.

The man took a handkerchief and dabbed his forehead and upper lip.

"Name's Jenkins. They hire me here so they don't git no trouble. You understand?"

"You gonna run after me if I cause some?"

The two men stared at each other.

"Was that not polite?" Sonny asked, and smiled. "I won't be causing any trouble here. I'm ex-law myself. Won't be here but a few days, max."

"That's good."

Sonny waited for more and the seconds piled up. He decided the man had used up his reserve of vernacular.

"Well then. I'm glad we understand ourselves," Sonny said, and slapped the arms of his chair.

"Wait a minute," the fat man said.

"Aren't we done yet?"

The man scowled and two of his chins bounced in vibration.

"What kind of law you come from? What with all them tattoos and thangs?" The man asked. He said *tattoos* like the word itself contained four syllables and was suspect.

"LAPD."

"That right? You mind if I check on that?"

"'Course not. Harold Coleman, look it up," he lied. He suspected that the man had not the mendacity or the connections to do such a thing. Sonny knew the guy was so far over his head he had forgotten which way he had come before getting lost.

The man wrote the name down, or pretended to, and nodded unsatisfactorily. Then he leaned back in his chair. The two men sat in silence, staring at one another.

"Does this *work*? Do people *seriously* get intimidated by this schtick?" Sonny asked, and waved his hand into the air.

"What we don't need here are some—"

"What you need here is some fucking *competence*. You didn't ask me to spell the name I gave you. You didn't ask me what years, what division, who my partner was. You didn't ask me if I had any weapons, and if so, could you see them or could I check them in for my stay here. You should have known my name from the front desk before you ever got me into your office. You haven't asked what my business is, or if you can assist in it. You didn't give the common courtesy one professional gives another regardless of how suspect he is on the other's motives, and there is *nothing* that makes one man suspicious of another that can't be taken away with kindness. You are an embarrassing hack and a bully who shouldn't be allowed to carry even the plastic *fucking* badge you ordered for this job," Sonny said, and stood.

The man looked back at him and his eyes blazed but he said nothing. He dabbed the sweat once again. Then he opened his mouth and began to speak: "If you would have given me the time—"

"I'm only here for a couple days. Stay the fuck away from me until then," Sonny said, and walked out of the man's office. He had no idea if it would work, but he meant every word of it. He walked to the front desk.

"Why wasn't that man here when I checked in?"

The man behind the desk asked, "Who?"

"The house dick," Sonny specified.

"*Oh.* Such colorful phrasing. Mr. Jenkins is only here on a part-time basis, sir."

"That figures. Nice place you run here," Sonny said, and footed it across the lobby and out the doors.

Harold Coleman lived in Culver City. Or he did four years ago. So Sonny drove the Mercury west in search of a partner lost.

Harold had lived in an apartment of the sort that had sprung about the southland after the war like children in a catholic family. It shared a courtyard with many other units, halved in a way so that all of the front doors more or less faced one another. Harold and his wife had been saving for a house near the coast, though apparently that wouldn't be happening now. Sonny had little reason to think that Harold would still be in the same apartment, but hoped still that if his former partner had left, his better half would still be stuck there.

He parked the Mercury on National Blvd and crossed the nearly trafficless street to Harold's old complex. The white, ranch-style fence was beyond a use of any sort and had been built only for design as its posts were spread wide apart and its height was hardly such at all. It protected the grass courtyard on which two women sat sunning themselves on towels. Sonny looked them over in the hopes of finding Harold's wife but continued looking longafter he recognized her absence. They were in bathing suits though no water was present and wore sunglasses that gave them bug eyes, which somehow did not diminish their appeal. Sonny briefly considered his desperation before looking for apartment 8.

All of the doors were painted red in the complex and Sonny knocked on number 8 and waited. He could have waited for some time staring at the welcome mat like he was. After he knocked a second time one of the ladies on the grass looked his way.

"You gonna keep knockin?" she called over to him

Sonny looked at them and said nothing.

"'Cause if you are he aint gonna answer. He's got something called a *job*. Maybe you've heard about it."

She looked at her friend and they giggled.

Sonny thought about his options. He had already been seen, there wasn't any hiding that.

"Well now, how is it you know so much about me?" Sonny said in a strong southern accent he had long ago abandoned. It was an accent that he'd heard southern gentlemen use when he was a child. As he grew older he found that the title was untrue in more ways than one, but the affectation was disarming then as now. He smiled.

"Well, if you had a *job*, you wouldn't be knockin on somebody's door at near noon on a Tuesday afternoon in clothes that look like you been wearin em for three days, now would you?"

"Actually, lovely ladies, I have been vacationing in Europe for a spell and am looking for a Mr. Harold Coleman, whom I used to be acquainted with. Would either of you ladies know his whereabouts?"

The two birds looked at each other quickly and began talking in low voices. The one who had yet to speak was clearly apprehensive while the chatterbox was near set to burst. Or so it seemed to Sonny. He rolled

his eyes behind his sunglasses.

"Does he still live here, ladies? And may I add that your skin is

looking positively brilliant under this fine California sun today. Some

people would say that March is too early for such a thing as sunbathin' but

after looking at you two I think more people ought to try it. You are

absolutely radiant."

Now they were both smiling. The truth was that he feared

blindness if he took off his sunglasses so white was the pair.

"Harold still lives there. He drinks too much, too," said the one

who had not spoken. She said it quickly, as if she was trying to best her

friend.

"Now isn't that a lovely voice you have." Sonny smiled at her.

Then: "So he still lives here, you say?"

"Oh yeah," said the chatterbox. "His wife left him a couple years

back. Walked right out on him and got into a car with another man. Me

and Rhonda here watched the whole thing." She nodded at her friend.

"Well, my oh my. That doesn't sound too pleasant at all, now does

it? Poor Harold." Sonny shook his head in mock concern, and continued:

"I *am* sorry to hear that. Does either of you two beautiful ladies know

about what time he returns from his work these days? I would so like to be

here and surprise him."

"Six o' clock or so. Pretty regular," said the chatterbox. Then she added: "He's a cop."

"Sometimes he doesn't come home though. Don't know where he goes then." She shrugged to display her lack of knowledge. "Or he comes home and drinks like a fish. We even heard him cryin' in there some nights. Kinda pathetic, you ask me," said the quiet one.

"You ladies have been most helpful," Sonny said. "I will surely come back this evening when I think it a more appropriate time to meet with Mr. Coleman. Y'all stay in that sun now, you're looking just about ripe as peaches." With that, Sonny tipped his hat and walked back to his car.

The blush exhibited on the cheeks of the two sunbathers was such that it momentarily eclipsed the burn laying in wait upon their bleached skin.

***

Sonny lit a Chesterfield in the car and drove west on Pico blvd thinking of Harold and how he would squeeze him. He would be home this evening or else he would be hanging out on Central Ave., he and his lilywhite self. Everyone down there knew he was a cop *and* a jazz fanatic so they tolerated him in the hopes their club wouldn't be rousted. That was the game. Harold and Sonny had never been close, but they had been partners.

And in that, there was a trust—not one of friends, per se, but something akin to professional courtesy.

Near the border of Santa Monica he found a greasy spoon and parked in the matchbox-sized lot. He sat at the counter and grabbed a discarded newspaper that lay nearby. There were three other people in the joint. It looked like that was about all it could handle. A couple sat in the corner in a black plastic booth one next to another, rather than facing each other. Like they'd rather hold hands than look at one another. The last customer was a small man sitting three stools down from Sonny and smoking a cigarette. The cluttered ashtray in front of him was alibi enough. His hair hung about his face like it disliked his scalp and he wore a dark line of freckles across his nose. Sonny glanced over at him once and that was enough. Sonny decided that the man looked like he was born nervous, yet there was something familiar in his ferretlike demeanor.

The cook eventually came from between double doors which led to the kitchen and took Sonny's order. A fried egg sandwich, biscuits and gravy, and coffee. Sonny opened his paper. Nothing interesting was happening. Nothing was ever interesting in the newspaper. They could write an article about a man with three heads pissing on the pope while reciting De Sade and make the damn thing unreadable. There were movies out starring people you wouldn't want to spend five minutes with, politicians lying about their ambition, and human interest stories that weren't interesting. And a sale at Sears, Roebuck. That was the newspaper.

One thing Sonny had learned between his time on the force and in the war was that people didn't give a shit about what was happening unless it affected them or their wallets. And then they cared a lot and expected you to do something about it. News is abstract, but the eviction notice or dead brother brings with it an unwanted glimpse into reality and raises questions about fairness best left to philosophers. It was unnecessary or painful. That's it.

He sipped his coffee. Apparently it had been sitting around since 1948. He sipped it again to get used to it. He dumped cream and sugar in the hopes he couldn't taste it. The flavor was like an unwanted chorus from a song you can't get rid of.

The egg sandwich was better than plastic. The biscuits and gravy weren't moving on their own. They were nothing like Tennessee, but thankfully they didn't resemble Los Angeles, either.

Throughout his meal, the jumpy guy a few stools down kept staring at him. The couple had left, still next to one another, Sonny presumed.

He swallowed the bite of his sandwich and looked at the nervous man.

"I know you, chief?"

The guy jerked his neck like a tic but said nothing.

"Look. I love staring at other guys, too. But I'm taken. And ya know—a couple less cups of coffee this morning mighta been okay."

The recognition of hypocrisy had never been Sonny's strong suit.

"Tweet-tweet," the man chirped.

Sonny had stopped eating now and turned his body and faced the man. "Beg your pardon," he said.

"He's got birds now, birds now. Tweet-tweet."

The man spoke as if to another person altogether.

"Look, boy genius. I'm eating my sandwich. Take the act somewhere else."

"Doesn't remember. He's got birds now on his neck and he doesn't remember," the greasy man said to himself. Out loud.

If there were pieces to be put together at this point, Sonny felt like the undiagnosed retarded kid in kindergarten.

Then the cook walked out.

"This guy buggin you?" he asked Sonny.

"Matter of fact, yeah. He's been a bother since he was born. His mama shoulda raised the part of him that ran down her leg. It'd be more useful."

The cook smirked and looked at the greasy man.

"Shiv, I told ya to keep to yourself. Ya bug anyone and you're out. You know the rules."

He moved his thumb in the direction of the door like they were playing charades.

The cook looked at Sonny and said in the way of explanation, "He's been good lately. Really. I don't know why you bug him."

"He's got birds now. Birds," Shiv said.

"The fuck he talkin about?" The cook asked Sonny.

"My neck."

The cook looked close and saw what he saw and looked at Shiv again.

"The man's got tattoos. That bug you?"

Shiv looked out the window and smoked his cigarette. He was saying something but neither man could hear it. He moved then, suddenly, and shifted three chairs left. The furthest stool available. He slid his ashtray with him.

"F-fill it up. The brim and such. To the brim," Shiv said, and pointed at the coffee cup. It should have been obvious to anyone with vision that the man needed more coffee like Los Angeles needed another actor but the cook filled it anyway.

"Your last one," the cook said, to make himself feel better. He smiled at Sonny then. He was short and looked Italian to Sonny, but a lot of people looked Italian to Sonny.

He filled Sonny's mug without asking and Sonny looked at him like he had just run over his puppy. The cook put the check down and said: "just leave it near the register there if I'm not back. I got dishes to do."

Sonny couldn't imagine whose dishes needed to be done but nodded nonetheless. He finished his sandwich and drank his coffee like he was dared to. He left the cash with the bill on the register. When he left he noticed the greasy man, Shiv, was beginning to leave the establishment as well. Sonny got in his car and drove off.

The Mercury sailed west towards the ocean. The greasy man was following him, of course, and couldn't have been more obvious about the enterprise if his Cadillac were a fluorescent pink and wore a lighted sign promoting DANCING GIRLS on the hood. Sonny exhaled and thought his options over. He knew that he was one stop at a red light away from the gas chamber given the wrong circumstances and spending the day dancing with a crazy man held no appeal. He remembered a cemetery near 20th street and floated in that direction in the hopes Shiv would forget he was crazy.

The gates were open and the grounds empty. Graveyards are always empty, because everyone there is dead. He pulled over on one of the access roads and reached into the back seat. His jacket lay there and he foraged in the pocket and pulled the .45 automatic out. Without ever bringing it within sight of the windows, he slid the piece into the front seat and then into his front pocket. At worst, he would look like a necrophiliac, sprung from the waist down staring at gravestones.

He opened the car door and walked onto the tended grass. The sprinklers had recently been shut off and beads like tears lay heavy on the grass and his brogues sunk into the soil. Shiv had parked his car some fifty yards behind the Mercury and sat in it still. Sonny looked at the gravestones set about in some geometric order of the damned until he found a name he liked. Henry Kaufman. He knew a Henry from before the war, a school teacher from Cleveland if he recollected, and he was a good guy. A bit on the uptight side, maybe. He wondered what had happened to Henry. Then he looked down again at Henry Kaufman. 1906-1946. Sonny glanced at Shiv's caddy. It hadn't moved.

He decided to walk towards one of the larger crypts to see if Shiv followed. He adjusted his hat and saw that there was one such structure less than a hundred yards away and he strolled towards it with his hands in his pockets. The sun lay in bands of short shadow and crashed through tree limbs of thick foliage. Shiv followed him in his car. Not much of a walker, that Shiv. Sonny thought.

Upon reaching the crypt, Sonny looked at the door without any notion of how to open it. Truth was, he had never been in one of these things. The door was iron at his best approximation and as he pulled the lever guessed the weight at near forty pounds. It creaked like he was in a horror film. He heard the whistle of the bullet before the pang! on the door and looked then at Shiv and his car. The greasy man stood some thirty yards away and had exited his car and was resting his arms across its roof as he shot.

Sonny reached into his pocket then and sprinted towards Shiv. If there was one thing his colored past had taught him, it was that once the dance began most men can't hit a stationary target, let alone a moving one. He ran at Shiv and made ground at a rapid rate, shifting his path both left and right as randomly as he could. He didn't like the gunshots. The one thing he didn't want yet was attention and gunshots were about the only surefire way to bring that, even in a graveyard. Shiv kept shooting and missing. Sonny heard one whistle rightly by his head, but the rest may as well have been aimed at the dead about him. Finally Shiv was turning empty chambers and banged the roof of his car at his incompetence and opened the door and sat down. Sonny arrived without breath and Shiv.

was trying to turn the key in the ignition. Sonny opened the door and pointed his .45 so that it bent Shiv's ear.

"Quit it, wild man," he huffed. "You turn that key again and I don't play nice anymore."

Shiv tried the engine once again and it caught. Sonny twisted the revolver in his hand and thumped Shiv in the temple with the butt hard enough that he checked the greasy man's pulse upon his collapse. Sonny reached in and removed the keys. He pulled Shiv out of the car by his collar and dragged him the length of the grass to the crypt, his dead weight crushing the damp blades like an announcement.

Sonny slapped the little man twice and there was no reaction. He looked around and the place was still empty. Somehow. That wouldn't last. Apparently, the undertaker was dead here too. The knot on the side of Shiv's head had reddened and resembled the world's largest mosquito bite. As if the mosquito was a pterodactyl. He dragged Shiv into the crypt and laid him on one of the stone benches. Sonny looked at the man once more and still had no recollection. He looked like any two-time loser. Sonny frisked the body once and there was nothing of interest. The gun remained in the car. Sonny left the man there and pushed closed the iron door to the crypt.

Rifling through Shiv's car, Sonny took the snubnose revolver and the half empty pack of Lucky Strikes that lay on the seat. The glovebox was as empty as gloveboxes get. Some registration papers, five bullets. That was it. He walked around to the hood and opened it and with his knife, cut the plug wires and the ignition. He closed the hood and looked about. The graveyard was still as busy as a graveyard. He walked casually but with some urgency to his Mercury and tossed Shiv's car keys into the grass along the way.

Upon reaching the exit gate and seeing no immediate danger, Sonny exhaled in a way he didn't realize he knew.

7.

Sonny sat on Harold's stoop with the neck of a bottle of Four Roses whiskey in his right hand. Sonny saw Harold walking from the parking lot in the rear of the complex, head hung like it was a Monday. Though he had known Harold for more than a decade, the man's height still surprised Sonny when he saw him. Harold was 6' 4" and looked taller. His walk was all lope and stretch. Sonny pushed his hat back on his head for easier recognition and waited. As Harold approached he looked up and abruptly stopped his gait. He looked hard at Sonny.

"What the hell you doin' here?" He asked.

"Waiting for you to get home, honey," Sonny said, and raised the bottle in greeting.

"I could have you arrested."

"I get exiled to Mexico for four years and *you're* the one sore? This is the greeting I get?" Sonny asked.

"You know you're still wanted?"

"You still a cop?"

"*Barely*," Harold said. He and Sonny connected eyes with a smirk.

Neither man said anything for a spell. Harold removed his hat and rubbed his handkerchief over his forehead. As he pulled it away he looked at it in his palm like an answer was writ there. He looked to Sonny like he had never had a weekend, then began the process anew and squinted his eyes.

"What the hell, you all drawn up like a circus freak now? Tell me them things aint real."

Sonny looked over his chaotic arms and hands and the ink there as if he had never noticed them before. He nodded slowly and smiled and said: "They kept me from goin crazy down there. Go figure."

"You look like you *are* crazy."

Sonny had nothing for that one.

"So what's the big, bad outlaw want from me?" Harold asked.

"I hear you're flying solo these days," Sonny said, and smiled.

Harold's eyes pinched and then resigned themselves. "Gimme that rye," he said, and snatched the bottle Sonny held up. He fumbled with his keys for a moment and opened the door. They walked into the apartment, one behind the other. The first thing Sonny noticed were the empty bottles on the floor and clothes hanging over the arms of the couch. It looked like it hadn't been dusted since the Jurassic.

"Looks like the maid aint been by, huh?" Sonny said, upon viewing the inside of the place. Getting no response from Harold, he plowed ahead: "Still spending too many late nights over on Central, H?," he asked.

Harold looked at Sonny and broke the plastic seal and tilted his head back with the bottle. When he pulled it away some shot onto his chin. "You're still a heel," he said after he had swallowed. "Always were."

"Yeah," Sonny nodded. "And yet you still love me."

"Yeah, like gonorrhea." Harold tilted the bottle again.

Sonny smiled at the exchange and camaraderie. Like old times. He sat on the sofa printed in orange and yellow flowers and as he did pulled the .45 from the rear of his waistband and placed it on his lap.

"What the *hell?*," Harold exclaimed.

"I can't *sit* on the damn thing. Relax."

Harold walked into the kitchen and opened the fridge. "You want something to drink, since you're sittin in my friggin living room?"

"How about some water?"

"Water?"

"Water."

"With the rye?"

"No. Just water," Sonny answered.

"Jesus Christ. Yeah, alright. Water."

Harold walked back into the room with a bottle of Pabst Blue Ribbon and Sonny's water. He handed the glass to Sonny, who looked at it like he had never seen a plastic cup before.

"This okay to drink?"

Harold looked at Sonny. Then he took a hit from the bottle and followed it with a beer chaser. "Sonny," he said, "You and I both know that if you so much as *thought* that water I just handed you was tainted I'd be dead before you finished a sip." He looked at Sonny after this admission like he would rather be somewhere else than his own living room.

Sonny only smiled at him, as if some recollection of said language brought back a memory only he was privy to. Then he took a large sip of the water.

"Now there aint no guarantee you won't grow two heads tomorrow morning—this is LA tap water we're talking about here," Harold said. He waved his arm at the thought.

Sonny gave a short chuckle at the idea, and said, "Remember H, we're not punished for our sins but by them," and raised the cup of water in a faux cheers.

"What?" Harold asked, and took a drink anyway.

"It never gets any easier. You think, when you're young, that old guys got things figured out. That when you're their age, you'll know everything you need to know. Now we're that age. Look at us," Sonny said.

Harold said nothing to that. Simply exhaled and took a draft of beer.

"So be straight," Harold said, finally. "You here for Cohen or Big Vinnie?"

"Now why would I come back from a beautiful vacation in Mexico—a land of eternal sunshine and beautiful tanned women—to pull the puds of two wop lowlifes?"

Harold thought about that one a moment. He rubbed his chin. Then he answered: "For Katie. For *Betty*."

Sonny looked at Harold for a moment like he was not his old partner. Then Sonny leaned back on the couch and smiled and the moment forgotten. "She's grown up now," he said. "It's friggin crazy."

"You heard about Emma?"

"I heard it. Any leads?"

"Sonny. You aint a cop anymore. Leave it alone. You're like that guy, what's his name, Mudjaw? Redneck cracker they caught down in Mississippi. Or Tennessee. Your old stompin grounds. You two are probably related. Anyway—"

Sonny looked at Harold like he *had* grown a second head.

"Yeah. Guess you're not up on the current affairs so much."

"Mexico aint exactly the hot spot for the regular, y'know? Anyway, now I can do things without all the bureaucracy and paperwork," he said, and smiled again.

"You think I like this? You comin into my house, wanted by the LAPD and talking like this? Man, I don't need this shit."

Sonny lit a Chesterfield and exhaled toward the ceiling. He said nothing.

"We got no leads. We got nothin. We thought maybe this guy from Downey—but nothing."

"What about Shiv? That ring a bell?"

Harold laughed. "Shiv Schule? Yeah. Hell. We sent his brother to Quentin before the war. You don't remember?"

Sonny shook his head and smoked his cigarette down.

"He was the kid they caught doin that bank job on Western in the clown suit all hopped up. He had the red nose and everything. Anyway, he caught a twenty jolt. We knew Shiv was there too but we couldn't pin him. I heard he was running wetbacks to Bakersfield and central Cali." He shook his head slowly, and finished: "Not my business anymore."

Sonny took all this in. "Y'know, I *do* remember the clown suit," he said finally. "Just not the name. Or a brother. Anyway, you may want to check the crypts in that cemetery on 20th tomorrow. He may still be there." He grinned and continued: "little fucker shot at me today. He couldn't have hit me if I was holding a bullseye over my chest, but I didn't care for the attention."

"What with your sterling reputation and all. Damn Sonny—20th is Santa Monica, you know that. They can handle that shit. That's not our jurisdiction, not our problem."

"Whatever. I won't be in town long enough to get fingered."

Harold thought about that and said nothing. He drank from both bottles. He looked hard at Sonny. His tattoos. His tan. Barely the same man until you talked to him. "You know I shot a kid?" he asked, and shook his head as if the thought itself were unwanted. "A little black kid—he was in 3rd grade," he continued, talking now to the fates as much as his guest.

Sonny breathed slowly out of his nose and thought of many things to say but said none of them. Finally: "That why you're at a desk now?"

"One and the same," Harold said, and took a huge pull of the whiskey. "He was eight," he explained. "In this garage a block from a 187. We were doin a sweep and he got scared and tried to open the back door and he had this bike mirror in his back pocket. It was dark. I thought— well, anyway. He spent two days in the hospital and I stayed with his parents there. He never came to." Harold wiped quickly some moisture at the corner of his left eye. "Gerald. Gerald Washington was his name," he finished. "His parents must've told me twenty times how good he was at math. About how—," he stopped, and look at Sonny as if there were no words to finish the sentence.

"I'm sorry, H. That's no good." Sonny lit another cigarette and looked at his old partner the way old partners do. Eyes full of mingled empathy and sarcasm.

Harold stood up, his body language all capital letters.

"You wanna know why you never cut it as a cop, Sonny?"

Sonny raised his eyebrows. "So this is about *me* now?" he asked, and waved his cigarette towards Harold. "Sure. Enlighten me," he said, smiling.

There was a tear streaming down Harold's right cheek that he did not wipe away. Sonny wished that he had.

"Because when I'm the best cop in a partnership, somethin aint right. You were tough. The whole friggin city knew that. But you were never a *good cop*. You would always rather bust heads and crack wise than do the footwork." He shook his head then and looked like he would continue but did not. Took a hit of the rye instead.

"Yeah," Sonny said, with his arms out in a sign of resignation. "You got me. I'm a bad guy." He smirked, and continued: "I'm sorry about the kid though. Really. That's a bad break, H."

Harold nodded in agreement. There was nothing else to do.

"And Celeste?"

Harold's face pinched like he had stubbed a toe. Then it cleared and he looked away, towards the kitchen and the deep shadows from the western sun nearly set. "What *about* Celeste?" he asked.

"She leave 'cause of shootin' the kid?"

Harold thought that one over. The fact was that there wasn't much to think over, but Harold wasn't much of a thinker. And Truth is often darker than first realized and no amount of rationalization can ease that. Finally, he simply shook his head, the act neither an admission nor refusal, and further diminished the bottle of rye.

Sonny said nothing and instead stood from the couch and stretched. He put the handgun in the waistband of his trousers and walked through the apartment. He peered into the bedroom and down the hallway and then walked into the kitchen. It was the shape of a square and had a black and white linoleum floor. The counters were a white and mint green tile combination.

A specked linoleum table framed in chrome sat near the windowed back door. Sonny turned on the overhead fan and walked the kitchen and opened the door. It led to an alleyway and had two steps leading down and a small clothesline that was little used and had begun to rust. Sonny flicked his cigarette into the alley and turned back into the kitchen. He flipped one of the chairs around at the kitchen table and sat there facing the open doorway.

"It's better in here. Got some crossdraft goin on. Not so stuffy."

No response.

"Whaddya got to eat?"

Harold appeared in the doorway with the bottle of rye. It was still some three-quarters full but Sonny knew that would be short lived. Harold looked at him with no small level of disgust and said nothing. Then some manner of his place in the scheme of things occurred to him and he answered: "I got some hot dogs."

"Ok. Sounds good. So tell me. They ever find anything else on Betty's murder?"

"Do you mean are *you* still the main suspect?" Harold grinned as he said it, and filled a pan with water and placed it on an already lit burner.

"No, shithead. I figured that. Did they ever find anything else at the scene? Besides my prints and Vince's."

"Nope," Harold said, and shook his head. "They didn't. And Vince had an airtight alibi, you know that."

Both men went about the business of nothing certain, neither looking at the other, neither thinking terribly deep thoughts, neither giving any indication that he was in the presence of another.

Moments passed like sandy thighs.

"You still think I did it, don't you?" Sonny asked, a hint of surprise not hidden in the tone.

Harold said nothing to that. He looked at the black and white linoleum floor like it was a design he was trying to memorize. Then he spoke in a whisper: "I always wondered why your story didn't pan out, that's all, Son. But I never thought you *did* it. I could just never put the whole thing together, y'know? But, I mean, c'mon. It was *Betty*, for chrissakes. She was the only thing on the friggin planet you gave a shit about. Her and Katie."

Sonny looked back at him and drank his water.

"And I still don't think it was Vince," he continued, speaking normally. "Probably some new guy just come out west tryin' to impress Bugsy and Mick. But then why wasn't there no prints? Mob guys, particularly new mob guys, just aren't that careful." He looked at Sonny for an answer.

"H, you know we had just collared three of his boys in that sting downtown. He found out from Vince that Betty was, *y'know*, and figured they could pinch us that way. I still don't know if the thing was a hit or if it just went bad. Anyways, it's ancient history. She aint comin *back*," he said. Then he looked to the ceiling as if there were none and whispered something unintelligible.

"We're some sorry sacks, you know that?" Harold asked, and placed four hot dogs in the boiling water on the stove.

Sonny smiled weakly at Harold.

"You hear about Bugsy?" Harold asked.

"Two in the head, more in the chest and neck, right? My paycheck told me about that," Sonny answered. "He thought it was funny. So did I, come to think of it," he said.

"Right at his squeeze's house," Harold said.

"That was for fuckin up the Flamingo, and the rest of Vegas, we talked about that a long time ago. We knew that shit was comin down the pipe at some point."

"Yeah, well, *he* didn't," Harold answered, and nodded at the truth of it. "You shoulda seen Mickey though. You hear about *that*? You'da loved it," he said, and looked at Sonny for some confirmation.

He shook his head from side to side and looked towards Harold, eager for the skinny.

"The friggin guy just went berserk about Bugsy. He walks into the goddamn Roosevelt with pistols blazing and shoots em into the ceiling, hair all crazy. You imagine that? The guy's got 25 hats in hat boxes back home and he leaves his place with his hair looking like he stuck his finger in a socket and no suit jacket. Anyway, so he's screaming and tells the assassins, that's what he called em, *assassins*, that they got to come down or else. Or else what? He's gonna shoot the guys just for comin down! But nobody comes down, right? And he won't go up, and he knows *we're* showin up so he hightails it out like a little girl. We shoulda just let 'em be. Let them lowlifes just shoot each other all up, knock each other off." He smiled at the memory and continued: "I wish I hadda picture. He's runnin it now though, better than Bugsy ever did. Got his hand in so many pockets it aint funny," Harold said, and then looked at Sonny like it was.

Sonny had worn a smirk throughout the bulk of the story and wore it still as Harold looked at him. Then he looked out the back door and into the alley that had begun to blacken down. He exhaled a lungful of smoke in that direction.

"Vince is going off the board—take that how you want," Sonny said. The admission sat there for a moment like a burp in the conversation.

"I'm gonna tell somebody and save a greaseball? C'mon," Harold said. Then he waved his hand at the ridiculousness of the thought. He raised the bottle in Sonny's direction as an offer to which Sonny shook his head and sipped his water.

"You bring my brand over and won't drink none?" Harold asked.

Sonny scratched his forehead with his thumb and scrunched his brow while the cigarette burned before it. Brought his hands out in mock resignation.

"How long you been on the wagon then?"

"Awhile now. Since a few months after Betty. Down in Mexico."

"Well, if there's anybody that needed it, it was you. You were fuckin nuts half the time. You miss it?"

"Every sip you take."

"I won't tell," Harold confided, and smiled.

"Naw," Sonny said, before growing silent. Then finally: "I aint fuckin this up."

Harold sipped the rye and made eye contact with Sonny then.

"Tell me about Mexico," he said.

8.

Sonny thought about the request a moment. He dragged his smoke. He sipped his water. Harold walked to the kitchen table and sat in the chair opposite him. Were it all for dramatics it was impressive enough, but Sonny had thought over the specifics. Finally he spoke: "Okay. I'll spill. You got some coffee?"

Harold's smile was one born of curiosity and grown wider by the bottle. "Yeah, sure," he said, and walked to the stove to begin another process anew. He pulled the steaming hot dogs from their pan and tossed them into buns softer than concrete.

"I contacted Sanchez when I got down there. Remember Sanchez?" Sonny asked.

"The dealer, yeah," Harold answered. "You still take mustard and kraut? I feel like I'm wearin a skirt here."

"Yeah, plenty of both," Sonny answered offhandedly, and continued: "So Sanchez, I let him know that I was available and all. He sent two fronts to check me out. Like LAPD is gonna send somebody down past Tijuana, right? Anyway, they get me at this coastal cantina

that's empty as your head and start askin' me these questions. Like am I

fired. Why am I in Mexico. That shit. One of them doesn't like his job, he

doesn't wanna believe me, so he starts actin tough. Like *I* oughta be afraid

of *him*. He's pulled like what, probably two guys—with a gun, no less. So

I tell them I'm gonna hit the head knowin the dumb fuck's gonna follow

and when he walks in the door to check on me I stick his head in the toilet.

Nothin to get ya goin quite like a urine shampoo. Anyway, I take his own

gun and blow his head into the shitter after I demoralized the little fucker

and then I exit the stall like it aint nothing. The other guy comes along and

asks where his partner is, like *I'm* supposed to keep tabs. I tell him once,

like the *nicest* guy around, forget about him. He aint worth missin. But

the guy persists. Like an amateur. So I tell him to check the bathroom. He

pulls his piece and starts walkin' over there, motioning with me to follow.

So I follow him. He walks in, all of a sudden I got two fuckin morons dead

and bleedin' in the only stall in the place. That's Mexico for ya. Anyway,

I walk out to the bartender, who hadn't moved, by the way, and tell him to

tell Sanchez that he needs me like fuckin England needed Churchill if these

are his boys. At first the guy dummied up, but when I showed him what

he had to clean, he figured it out. Next week, Sanchez was visiting with me

alone. That was it. It started then."

He paused to light another chesterfield and exhaled and stared out into the alleyway.

"At first Sanchez was sore at me for takin out two of his goons like that. I told him that he should get better goons. Finally he laughed and then we were alright. So I start doing odd jobs for the guy, y'know? Anything to keep my mind off the shit that happened here. Off Betty. I escort him places, sometimes his daughter. Social events. When he asks me to send a visual, it's easy stuff. Broken bones and a message, y'know?"

Harold nodded that he did, and handed Sonny a mug of steaming coffee and a plate with his dogs. Then he bent once and fell into his own chair, a gathering of aging knees and liquor.

"Thanks, H. I appreciate it. So it's maybe 3, 4 months in that I finally get some meat jobs: a car bomb, a whack at an opera house—good stuff. Then one of his own starts gettin a little cranky and he has me make a little art project out of the guy. And I see this carnival crossing across the flat desert not far from where I am and I think, when the hell was the last time I saw a circus? What's the difference anyway, between a circus and a carnival?"

Harold didn't have the answer to either question and looked the part.

Sonny sipped his coffee and swallowed, tipped the mug towards Harold as a sign of appreciation. Bit into his dog and began talking with his mouth a concoction of sauerkraut and pressed meat.

"I don't know neither. Anyway. Never. I aint never been to the circus. So I go and watch some of the stuff—elephants, trapeze, all that shit. And I'm walkin around the tents and such and there's this guy doing tattoos. He's got lots of em himself—not as many as the tattooed man they had there, but still more than you. So I watch what he's doin' with this gal on her back—he's drawing this ship with a full mast and sails and such, and I start thinkin about gettin one. I was missin Betty every friggin moment at this point even though I was tryin not to—and so I had him put the teardrop on. Right then, when he was done with the woman. And it hurt, but it was a good hurt. Like it's supposed to hurt somehow, y'know?"

Harold tipped the bottle back. It was half empty now. Then he placed it on the linoleum between his feet and stared at Sonny, rapt.

"And so I kept gettin em. I like the hurt of it. I like that you can't take 'em off. Sanchez, after the first couple, he asks me what am I doin, but I told him that it aint none of his damn business. And he listened. I don't know why. So anyway, I kept doin jobs for the guy and after each one I'd track down the carnival and get some more work done. And it kept me busy. All of it."

He sipped his coffee.

Harold looked at Sonny as he finished. He slapped his knee once and asked, "So why come back now, Sonny? Why not start over. You're already in Mexico. What about the Caribbean? Hey, I heard Cuba is nice these days. You can always find work. I mean, y'know?"

"I don't know, H. I mean, for Katie, 'course. You know that. I was always gonna come back to check on her and Emma. But I just got the feeling that I should head back and take care of some unfinished business. The last decade has been rough. The streets and the mob boys with you, the war, Mexico. Betty. A lot of pain and bullshit in those years. I was hopin' I could come back here and finish the thing off. Take Vince and call it a wash. *Then* maybe start over somewhere."

Harold said nothing and sipped at the whiskey. Then he smiled and spoke with a vicious sarcasm: "White picket fence, couple of rugrats, *yeah*, I can see it."

"Okay, supercop," Sonny retorted, then added: "Be on the lookout for those 8-year old future math teachers with bike mirrors, now."

Harold sat back in his chair like he had been slapped.

Sonny figured it was time to continue his story.

"So anyways, I told Sanchez a couple weeks back that I'm gonna be leavin and he freaks out. Like I'm a part of the family or something. I tell him I don't get it. But he tries to convince me to stay, like he's in danger if I leave. I tell him that he had imbeciles guarding him before and he was fine, so not to worry. So then he gets mad. He threatens me. Which I am *not okay* with. You know this."

Harold looked at Sonny with a cringing aggression, all angle and solitude, like a kicked stray.

Sonny smiled then, really smiled, for the first time in the story.

"So I borrowed his car and came up anyways."

"You stole his car?" Harold's eyes lit at the notion.

"He won't report it."

"What'd you do?" Harold was slurring now, and smiling again, stuck in the story like a bear in the zoo.

"I took him to this spot where I said there was this new source willing to deal and I drop him off. I had worked a couple of these so I figured it'd work. And we're in the middle of the desert. He looks at me like, What the fuck? I tell him to cool his heels, the kid will get here. Then I go back to the car to get the matches and I start the thing and run him down like roadkill. He ran for a bit, but I clipped him once and came back for him. Then I drove up here. End of story. He's still on the hardpack somewhere in fuckin Nowheresville, Mexico, gettin pecked at by vultures." He shook his head and finished: "And there but for the grace of God..."

"You killed *Sanchez?*" Harold asked, as if the thought were unimaginable then or now.

Sonny said nothing but stood up and filled the doorway to the alley. "He needed killing," he said. "He was a waste of space. H, there's an awful lot of people on this ball that don't deserve to be here. Period."

Harold tipped back the whiskey and said nothing.

"You remember that kid we caught in Santa Monica after he had raped and cut up that little girl at the apartment complex? That was one helluva fall that boy took. Not bad enough though."

"Yeah, 'course," Harold answered, and his shoulder ticked at the admittance.

"She was what, 11, right? What was her name? I swore I wouldn't forget her name. *Fuck*."

"It was Twylla, wasn't it?"

Sonny took it in and let it wash over him. Twylla. Beaten and raped and sodomized behind her own apartment building after walking home from school by a 17-year old dropout. It had bugged Sonny then, much more than the organized crime that he had been used to dealing with, and thinking about it bugged him still.

"That kind don't deserve a trial. They don't deserve their next breath."

"Maybe," Harold answered and stared at him. "But aren't you just the guy who spent four years working for a notorious drug dealer and on the lam for allegedly killing your wife?" He asked, with surprising clarity given his state.

Sonny sighed and waved his hand at the question as if it were a pesky fly. "Yeah, I guess so," he answered, incompletely. He removed his hat and ran his hand through his slickedback hair and grinned. "My hypocrisy," he said, "surprises even me sometimes."

Neither man said anything. The night was yet young but a conclusion had been struck that Sonny nor Harold had writ for it. It hung there like the world's worst curveball.

"So tell me about what you've been up to," Sonny said, and drank some water in an attempt to put behind him those things that served as reminders of a past he wanted little remembrance of but knew fully that he would never escape.

The evening drew to a close near midnight. Harold had passed out in his chair, the bottle of Four Roses nearly empty. His head was reared back in such an awkward fashion that when Sonny gazed upon him it was only the twin bores of nostril that he saw. Sonny was on his fourth cup of coffee and was beginning to wonder if he would ever need sleep again. Before Harold had passed into his present state Sonny learned that Mickey would be attending most of the Stars games at Gilmore Field once the season started, and the season started in two days. Mickey liked to sit in the dugout or right above it during games as if he belonged though in truth Sonny suspected he was allowed to stay because nobody had the nerve to ask him to leave. Vince would accompany him, Sonny was sure of it.

Sonny drew a tall glass of water from the sink and stood it on the table not far out of reach from Harold, as he knew his former partner would awake parched and dizzy in the morning light. Then Sonny walked out of the back door which led to the alley and footed it across the street and there the Mercury sitting attendant. He drove off into the starless black Los Angeles night vainly planning the days before him like a map unreadable so unclear was the design of one fate to the next.

***

He parked his ride in the lot, which was nearly empty, and sat in his car amid the silence.

Regardless of what travels await this life, night silence remains the same. At times crickets blanket the unheard, or the blare of humanity imposes, but always in the absence squats silence, as black and hopeless as twin gunbores.

Sonny sat in his car and listened to the quiet of it though he couldn't help but tap his foot against the floorboard because of the coffee. And he had to take a piss on account of the same.

Finally, he walked to the rear entrance of the hotel and there through a swinging glass door and he stood at that elevator and wondered.

Chuck was seated in the elevator sound asleep, his snore ripping through the corridor in a stuttered consistency.

Sonny tapped him on the shoulder.

"Chuck."

The boy woke in two stages, the first a haze of semireality and the second one of embarrassed alertness. He snorted as he stood.

"I can't believe you're still here, kiddo. Eighth floor, please. I'm hoping to get to my room before sunrise."

"Yessir," the kid said, and ran his hand across the whole of his face as if it were a mask. "Working a double," he stated.

"Anybody else in my room tonight?"

"If you mean the girl, yessir."

"Any auditions today?"

"No sir. I slept until noon. I was tired," he said. He looked at Sonny to gauge whether tired was an appropriate emotion to feel.

"Well. The best in life keep funny hours, son. I once knew a man who could work all day and all night long but had to get a catnap every three hours. Aint no figuring. Me, I'm all over the place," Sonny said.

"No sir."

"No sir, what?"

"Yessir, people do sleep some strange hours."

"Back in Tennessee, I could never sleep, come summers. You would lay there buck naked with nothing but a sheet and sweat through the thing before you ever caught sleep. Don't never travel to the South in the summer, son. Tennesse sucks in the summer."

Chuck looked at him like he needed a script for the next line.

"What is it, Chuck?"

"You're not gonna tell anyone, 'bout my sleeping and all?"

"What, that you fell asleep at one in the morning on the job you been working for twelve hours with no customers around? You did exactly what you should be doing. Hell. I'da been asleep soon as I took the job, I was you."

Chuck smiled quickly, then recovered and the two men looked collectively at the numbers above them. The gold arrow was pointing at the number 4.

"My God," Sonny exclaimed.

"We're getting there, sir."

"Bet you say that to everyone."

"No, you're my first one," Chuck said innocently.

Neither responded to that explanation though a universe of comebacks sprang into Sonny's mind.

"I always thought I'd die in an elevator," Sonny said, flatly.

Chuck said nothing but smiled at him.

"No, seriously. Don't you feel like real time doesn't really pass in these things?"

"Actually, I feel like a lot of time passes for me in elevators," Chuck answered.

"Well, yeah. In *this* elevator we may lose a day."

As the arrow reached 8 Chuck pushed the hammer down on the lever.

Sonny walked out of the elevator and turned and said: "Dust and bones, kid. None of it matters. See ya tomorrow." Then he turned before Chuck could answer and walked to his room, feeling like he had played the part of junior philosopher all day and felt illfitted for the part.

9.

His key turned silently and he entered the dark room. The curtains were splayed open and light fell in a soft geometry across the carpet, all skewed angle and warped shadow. He toed his brogues off by the heel and walked to the bed. Katie lay there on top of the covers, a book halved near her right hand. He stood and watched her breathe. In and out, the rhythm of it oceanlike. Then he picked up the book and looked at it. It was *A Rage to Live*, by John O'Hara. A hardback covered in the translucent film that accompanied the possession of a library. On the first page it held a card and announced that it was the property of the San Diego Public Library. Then he thumbed through the pages and read a tiny piece of it, a small paragraph that held nothing of the truth contained within, because that is what people do when they pick up a book without any intention of ever reading it. He placed the Ace of spades playing card that passed for a bookmark back into a fold of the book's substantial mass. Placed it on the nightstand.

He looked at the couch but knew that there would be no sleep for him now. He walked to the bathroom and there disrobed, placing the .45 automatic on the sink. He looked at his reflection, the hollows of his eyes rimmed in black. His stubble bordered on the patchy birth of a beard. And below it, running across his substantial collarbones and bookended with nautical stars, the announcement: *no future, no past.* The words were backwards in the mirror but held no confusion for him. Sonny ran a finger over the banner and then the stars that scarred his taut skin. He caught his own eye again and felt the stubble on his chin and began to run the shower.

When he had finished, he shaved, and, realizing he had not brought his bag into the bathroom, and walked into the room with a towel tied about his waist.

He closed the bathroom door quietly and entered the darkness, estimating the given space to the couch. Katie sat up on the bed as he attempted to tiptoe in silence.

"Sorry kiddo. Didn't mean to wake you," he whispered.

"I was barely asleep. I'm just glad you're back." Katie smiled. Her hair jutted out from the left side of her head as if it were frightened.

"Yeah. Listen, I'm just gonna—"

Sonny pointed towards the couch as if it were an ending to his sentence. Katie reached out from the bed and turned on the bedside lamp. Then she stopped him as he passed. She placed her tiny hands on the bridge of his shoulders and sat him on the bed like a puppet.

"You have *so many* tattoos now," she said.

"Yeah. Ummm. Look—"

Sonny tried to stand but she reseated him with a finger on his shoulder. It was a small finger. It shouldn't have weighed on him like that. Just three digits with a painted nail like an exclamation mark. She began tracing the fractal designs inked about his skin. There was a Celtic cross on his back which she circumnavigated the whole of and then the striped design of a tiger across the rear of his ribcage. Her fingers ran the stripes vertically as if she were drawing them. They moved down his back onto a small horizontal stretch that resembled his home state of Tennessee and below that the dancing bones of a skeleton. Her fingers worked their way up again and onto a bicep and there a girl reclining in a martini glass. About her lay playing cards strewn about and a bottle with XXX on the label. On a banner below the base of the glass, *Man's Ruin*.

"Kinda looks like me, the girl in the glass," she said.

And it did, too.

"Kinda looks like a lot of birds, Katie."

When her two hands found themselves flirting with the twin swallows on his neck, he stood abruptly though he had no explanation for the action.

"I think they're great," she said and smiled.

Sonny looked at her like she might bite.

"Really," she reiterated.

"I need them," he answered, lamely.

With that he walked away feeling like a little boy in a whorehouse. He was excited to be there, but knew that he really didn't have any idea what he was doing.

"Thank you for coming back," she said when he had disappeared into the other room.

He stopped then and turned.

"Baby. Of course. I was *always* coming back. I'm sorry it took so long."

Then he leaned his head into the doorframe and said: "Had I known your mama wasn't around, I'da come around a lot sooner."

"Yeah." That was all she said. Then she looked down at the bed like she was still 16.

"I saw Harold today," Sonny said.

"Yeah?"

"Same old Harold."

"Didya get any info from him?"

"Is that what I was doing, getting '*info*'?" Sonny asked, with a smirk full of sarcasm.

"You're no fun," she said, and threw a pillow in his direction.

Sonny stood in the doorway in an undershirt and his long boxer shorts adorned with horseshoes. He wanted a drink. Instead, he lit a Lucky Strike that had been Shiv's and blew the smoke at the ceiling. He wondered what Shiv was doing at that moment.

"What's the book about?" He motioned towards the bed with his chin.

She picked it up and looked at it like she had not seen it before. Then said: "It's about this girl, Grace. About her growing up and stuff," she said.

"Huh."

"She thinks about sex a lot. Very forward thinking for the time."

"And what time is that?"

"Right before the first war. 1917, I think."

"Sex makes for good books, that right?"

"Yeah, it's swell," she said, and placed it on the bed beside her.

Sonny smiled and turned back into the living room and then the deck. The wind was whirling on the 8th floor and his ash seemed to have a mind given its own inclinations.

Katie followed him out there in the sweater and skirt she had fallen asleep in and immediately began rubbing her shoulders for warmth.

"You realize that it's, like, what, probably 65-70 degrees out?" Sonny asked, without looking at Katie.

"Do you realize that way probably weigh twice as much as me?"

"At least," Sonny said. "But you're in a sweater and I'm in an undershirt."

"Didn't you always have this argument with Betty? I think I remember that."

Sonny didn't answer at first. Instead, he looked the lights of the city down and the cars passing singly like they were lost from the rest of the pack. Then he smirked at Katie and said: "Yeah. Yeah, sweetie. You remember that."

He reached over and tussled her hair like she was ten again.

"You miss her a lot still?"

"Just about every day. Sometimes, when it's not so good, it seems like she's all I think of," he said, and grabbed the iron bars and stared out at the city as if it were a thing that could be taken by will alone.

Katie nodded. "Yeah. I miss my mom, too. *And* Betty," she added.

"Yeah. If she just hadn't—," Sonny stopped his sentence and softly flailed his arm out into the morning to express his loss.

"I mean, how did *Vince* know?" Sonny continued. "The guy's such a friggin meatball. He couldn't make a decision on his own with an instruction booklet. I don't get it. He told me and Harold at the Trocadero one night when we came to talk to Mick. He tells us, *then* he has the two of them whacked. So I go home and find 'em both dead, and with my gun. You remember that revolver I used to keep by the bureau? I just don't get how that greaseball *knew*."

"What do you mean?" Katie asked. The wind was whipping her hair in circles so that she had hardly any face visible at all.

"Well. I guess it doesn't matter," Sonny lied. He dragged his cigarette and sent it sailing into the night, tip over end. They both watched it fall, carried weightless in the wind but with the embertip a lighthouse.

"We all *knew*, Sonny."

"Knew what, sweetie?"

"About Betty. I mean, *my mom* told me, but—"

Sonny turned quickly and grabbed her slight shoulders and shook them hard enough so that her head bobbed.

"*What?* You guys *knew?*" His face straightened into a look of shock, nearly without expression at all.

"Well, yeah. I mean, my mom, and most of the regulars at the Union Jack—she would see Billy...Bankley, Banken, Bankman, something like that, who worked in some club down there, you were always working—and you know how my mom couldn't..."

She looked at Sonny and stopped talking upon seeing his expression.

"Don't be mad at me, Sonny. I was only twelve."

Despite his anger, Sonny nodded and looked into the sky and spoke like he expected an answer: "Is there anybody in Los Angeles besides me who *didn't* know that my wife was fucking Scooter Webb?"

Katie didn't know what to do with that one.

Sonny exhaled loudly, all aimless rage and fatigue. Katie didn't move, recognizing that they were partners in discomfort.

He looked at her. "Hey," he said, "I'm sorry for grabbing you, sweetie." He looked at his hands then as if they were things entirely beyond his control.

"It's okay. Just don't be mad at *me*."

Sonny hugged her then, and kissed the top of her head.

"I'm not mad at you, sweetie. There's a lot of people I'm not real happy with right now, but you're not one of 'em. Hey, leave me alone for a few, k? I need some time out here."

Katie nodded, and walked to the sliding glass door and turned.

"I can come, right?"

"What? Come where?" Sonny asked.

"With you."

There passed a moment where he stared at her and she at him. If it was thought, it was hidden indeed.

"You bet," Sonny finally answered, and managed a mangled smile.

"How long then? Til we go?"

"Two, three days max."

Katie nodded once again and separated from him and made eye contact intended to bring cheer to a moment that would not allow any. She walked inside and he closed the sliding glass door behind her and Sonny sat then against the wall on the deck in that spring Los Angeles night. His thoughts were angry and sorrowful though he had relived that fated night more times than he cared to remember.

He wanted a drink then more than he could recall wanting one in a very long time. And suddenly, like the flip of a switch, he was chilled. He began rubbing his bare arms and rocking in place and finally gave out a short howl so swollen with pain and loss that it was bestial in its voice.

***

He awoke with the sun some hours later still on the deck with a cold that sat in his bones and would not leave with the dawning of a shirt and jacket. His fitful dreams had been filled with various scenes of him being pursued, though with the coming of the light from the eastern crease they lacked any relevancy and were soon forgotten.

He walked to the living room to find a note from Katie on the table. She would be studying at the library through the afternoon and had a game at the Union Jack that evening should he need her. He shook his head at the resiliency of youth and placed the note back on the table and shut the blackout blinds to create an artificial night. He found the .45 automatic in the bathroom where he had left it and shoved it under the pillow beside him after he crashed on the bed, where sleep was quick in its arrival.

10.

It was afternoon when he awoke. The day was warm and the curtains that led to the deck billowed softly with the breeze. He had left the sliding-glass door ajar that morning and as one thought to the next, Sonny immediately felt for his gun, and found it where he had left it.

He pomaded and slicked his hair in the bathroom and splashed water on his face. As he dressed himself, he decided on the day's itinerary, slightly altered by the revelation from the night before. He had to find this Billy Bankley or whoever he was first, and hope that Harold knew of him. Then he would head to Central that same evening. He outfitted himself in flatfront chino's and a blue sport shirt with white flecks, open at the collar and untucked. He shook loose from his suitcase the only sportcoat he owned, a two-button camel hair, and decided on the fedora for the trip. It was a soft brown with a red feather and a teardrop crown. He slanted it to the left as he placed it atop his dome. Then he walked to the mirror to ensure he would make the Central Ave. club scene. His brogues needed a shining and the whole of him could use a pressing, but he would fit in well enough. Besides the pigment issue, of course.

He crunched his hat low on his brow as he drove because of the sun's glare against the blacktop. Sonny had always been a night person, requesting night shifts when possible and eagerly accepting anything nocturnal thrown his direction. If he hadn't been such a night person maybe Betty wouldn't have gone around fucking jazz musicians, he thought. But he knew that blaming himself for his wife's infidelities was as pointless as licking his own ass simply because he had the time.

He rode Pico Blvd west and found the same greasy spoon as the day before. He parked his ride, grabbed a newspaper out of the trash can, and walked in. The place was jumping, comparatively speaking. About half of the tables were occupied. He removed his jacket and hung it on a hook near the entrance. Seated himself at the counter. There was a Mexican girl sitting on a stool behind the cash register. Sonny needed but a glance to wish he were the stool. Then the same cook walked out of the kitchen and gave Sonny a doubletake.

"Weren't you in here yesterday, mister?"

"Nope. Not me," Sonny answered, and lit one of Shiv's Lucky Strikes.

The man looked at Sonny, unsure. Then: "You're a riot, wise guy. What'll it be?"

"You remember what I got yesterday?"

"I remember you weren't here yesterday."

"It's all coming back to me now," Sonny said, and grinned.

"Yeah. Kinda."

"Just bring that."

The cook, who may still have been Italian, scribbled something on the pad he held. It may have been Sonny's order. It may have been a plea for help or a deeper meaning piggybacked onto a philosophical epiphany the cook had the night before. Either way, he took it into the kitchen with him. Sonny looked down the counter and there one other man, perhaps seventy. He was drinking coffee and his hands shook bringing it towards his mouth though he held it with both like it was the last egg in the world. Beyond him was the Mexi girl with her legs crossed. Her hair was impossibly long and her lips looked like pillows. Sonny wanted to touch them. In fact, every man who had ever been in the place wanted to run away with them. But they stayed there, right on her face. She was staring at Sonny. He pushed his hat back on his forehead and looked around. When he looked again, she was still staring at him. It was not a usual stare, the beehived housewife openmouthed "what has that man done to himself" kind of stare. It was one of a more prurient nature. And while Sonny recognized it, he doubted its existence just the same. Perhaps he had missed the headline. Maybe he should read that paper he held in his hands.

Maybe there in bold letters it would tell him that tattooed guys in their forties who resemble a severely beaten Cary Grant gone on a weeklong bender are all the rage for twentysomething Mexican beauties with pillows for lips. He looked down at the paper and it did not say that. Something about that ridiculous McCarthy character instead. Another fool in a history full of them. The cook placed a steaming cup of coffee in front of Sonny. He dragged his cigarette and carefully sipped his steaming coffee in the desperate attempt to avoid looking at her lips again. Failure never looked so good.

The food was brought over and it was better than the day before. Or perhaps he just wasn't thinking about how it tasted. In fact, that was it. He could almost smile at her, that's what a sap he was. When a couple brought their check to the register, she rang them in silence. They asked her a question and she wrote the answer on a pad of paper. Sonny stared at her and she at him after the couple left.

Then he finished his biscuits and gravy. A refill of coffee arrived and he didn't toss it down like shots of cloudy bourbon in a two dollar whorehouse. Somewhere in the back of his mind he found in himself the realization that the particular timing for such a venture was not ideal for meeting a woman, *even* a deaf woman. But he pushed that thought aside like it was a little kid trying to catch a foul ball at the stadium. When he had not finished his food but decided instead that he was somehow full, he pushed his plate away and finished his coffee. Lit another Lucky Strike. The cook brought the check and placed it on the counter.

"By the way, you seen Shiv?"

Sonny looked at the cook in a way that gave the man pause.

"Ummm. That guy who was in here yesterday with you? Little nervous guy?"

Sonny exhaled.

The man continued: "'Cause like, he left right after you and he didn't come in this morning."

"Nope. Maybe he went to the beach. Beautiful day, and all."

"Huh. Yeah. Well, okay," the cook said, and walked back to the kitchen. Sonny figured the cook thought something was fishy about it but he wasn't going to ask. Sonny figured that was wise.

He walked to the counter and grinned as he handed the girl his check and cash. She smiled back. Her skin was the color of tanned leather and she had a small scar underneath her left eye. But none of it mattered. Looking at her, it was as if there was a spotlight on her large brown eyes and lips. She could have had a two-inch mole on her cheek and it would have gone unnoticed. She didn't, of course, but she could have. She handed him his change and he held her hand a moment.

"Do you work tomorrow?" He asked, softly.

She nodded, then gently pulled her hand from his and held up three fingers.

"At three?"

She smiled.

"I'll see you tomorrow then," he said and turned to leave. Then he walked back to the counter and asked, "What's your name, sweetheart?"

She smiled at him and began writing on a pad near the register. She handed it to him and he read what was written: Miryea. He looked at her and read the name in the accented Spanish he had learned. She smiled again and looked away and that was enough.

He turned and grabbed his coat from the rack near the door and exited. He started his car in the lot and drove around the corner and still had yet to breathe. Then he pulled into an opening near the curb and stopped the car and got out and jumped up and down twice and let loose an uneven hoot of the desperate. And though his joyous revelation was purely improvised and couldn't have been more honest, it looked for all the world to a bystander like a seizure or the mating dance of a spastic.

***

When Sonny had rediscovered his dignity, he drove east to National Blvd. and parked there. He knew he was early and was tired of waiting for

106

Harold already. He had no whiskey this time. He wondered how Harold would handle that, and decided to remedy the situation instead.

Sonny walked the block down and there a corner market and he entered smoking the last of Shiv's pack. The woman behind the register equaled Sonny's 230 lbs. if she didn't exceed it by half and had a tattoo of an anchor on her massive forearm. She smiled at Sonny with as many missing teeth as those intact and gave him a thumbs-up for reasons as murky then as now. Sonny looked down to avoid the inevitable conversation.

In the liquor section he picked out an eighth of Four Roses and then a pack of Chesterfields and walked to the counter.

"Be doin a little drinkin, willya?" She asked.

Sonny stared at the lady, unsure as to how to answer any question she might ask, and fearful that his answer might be the wrong one. She might bounce him like a basketball out on the sidewalk with one arm tied behind her back. She might smile at him again. It was a crapshoot of loss.

"Where'd you get all them tattoos?" She cackled.

"In a chair," Sonny answered, and smiled.

The lady laughed then like her livelihood depended on it, long and hard and with a slap of the knee. The rollers in her hair moved about like something living as her head bobbed to and fro.

"You think you're a funny one," she said. When she spoke, her left eye squinted as if the sun and its glare insisted it.

"No ma'am."

"Smart men ain't no use, you ask me."

"Do people ask you?" Sonny said, and nearly covered his mouth with his hand.

She stared at him then and grinned. The rollers in her hair shook.

"Well. Useful ain't something I'm called very often," Sonny said.

"I'll bet. All that whiskey you been drinkin."

Sonny looked past the woman at nothing certain and nodded. He felt as if he had joined some improvisation of the absurd and shook his head at the whole of it. He ripped open the pack of cigarettes and lit one because it was the most definite thing he could think of at the moment, despite the fact that he had to put down his other nearly spent cigarette to do it. He was smoking doublefisted just to avoid conversation. This is what it had come to.

Finally, she rung him and he paid and she handed him the bottle though not without pulling it back twice from his reach and laughing each time as if it were a thing she were witnessing and not doing.

When the swinging doors of the corner market shut behind him he breathed deeply the Los Angeles air and felt lucky to be alive. At least he wasn't her, he reasoned.

Upon reaching Harold's apartment complex he found the same two women sitting in chairs on the lawn though it was well past any useful time for sunbathing. They were chatting like a pair of cackling hens and had yet to notice Sonny. He walked instead behind the complex and into the alley and there to Harold's back door. One of Harold's bedroom windows had been left ajar and thus Sonny invited himself in. He removed the screen carefully and climbed in and replaced the screen, sliding it into its given tracks and making sure that the nail to keep it in place upon the sill appeared untouched.

***

It was near dusk as he pulled into his garage, and upon entering his house, Harold stopped abruptly and pulled his gun. The radio in his kitchen played *Mona Lisa* by Nat King Cole and it echoed throughout the apartment like the whisper of something obscene.

Harold held the gun near his ear and looked about the living room and quickly the hallway and then ruminated upon the doorway of the kitchen like he knew his fate lay there. He tiptoed like a moose in that direction, and then threw himself into the doorway with gun and arms extended and there in a chair hidden from normal view sat Sonny with a .45 automatic aimed at Harold's head.

"AAHHHH!" Harold gasped.

Neither man fired. Then Sonny started laughing fit to bust a rib and lowered his gun to cover his mouth. "You're the best, H," he said as the moment faded.

Harold exhaled slowly and dabbed at the sweat perched on his forehead. "FUCK," he said. "You're *such* an asshole. It's fuckin crazy. I mean, I always know it, and you still surprise me." Harold thought about shooting Sonny anyway, then quickly reordered his night into one of sanity.

Sonny continued laughing.

Harold reholstered his weapon and leaned in the doorway. He exhaled again. "What the fuck you want now, Sonny?" He asked.

"Okay. Here's the thing. I'm sorry about that, H. I mean, it *was* fuckin funny. But I just couldn't help myself."

Harold waved off the sentiment as if it were undeserved, but he was unconvincing. He said: "I'm over it. What?"

"I need some help on Central, and I don't know anybody in LA who knows more about Central than you. It's almost a compliment, so take it that way. Anyway, I found out that the deal between Scooter and Betty— it wasn't any mystery. Vinnie found out from some guy that works down there. Be honest with you, I don't ever think Mickey was involved at all—you know how I had roughed Vince up a couple times the months before. I mean, we thought it was Mickey 'cause we were leaning on him a bit, but now I don't think so. Anyway, I gotta check it out."

"So check it out. Why bug me?"

Sonny just looked at Harold.

"You didn't know about this, right H?" Sonny asked.

Harold looked at him in astonishment.

Sonny stood, gun extended. He spoke: "Because, I mean, if you had known about this all along—," he stopped there, letting Harold figure out the rest.

"Sonny. C'mon, now. We was both there when Vince told us about Betty and, well, you know. C'mon, man. We was partners! How could I know something like that!" He finished, and they looked at each other, man to man. It was Harold's face that sold Sonny, not his words. Sonny sat again, convinced, and waved the gun like it had words to accompany it.

"What? Okay. I'm sorry. Of course, I'll help you find Vinnie if he did Betty, but, I mean, what do you want from me?" Harold pleaded.

Sonny did not answer and instead slapped the table next to him in a playful fashion. "I been thinkin about something I told you yesterday. About Sanchez. It was this *scene*, H. I'm out there on this desert floor with not a sign of civilization anywhere. Like the fuckin wheel's never been invented. 'Cept the car. 'Course, you could argue that you don't see civilization anywhere in Mexico. Anyway, literally, *nothing*. Not a tree, no buildings—just flat until the mountains. And no roads—we were a good half mile from even a deserted road at that point anyway. And Sanchez, he's next to me, and he's gettin so pissed at me, it was funny. He was fuming and telling me to pull the car over. And I say: Over to what? but he doesn't think that's funny, and he tried to grab the wheel. So I take my piece out and shove it up his nose and push him against his own window. And while I'm doing this—I'm pretty sure at this point that he knew there was no pickup point—while I'm doing this, the guy starts insulting me, my mother, my wife, my country, everything. And I start thinking: This is the guy I been taking orders from? Whose cash I been saving? I been killing other assholes for this asshole? So I decided right then to kill him. I mean, I *knew* I was going to anyway. That had been the plan. But it was business. Now the fucker was making it personal. We had a trunk full of zeroes, for chrissakes. And I almost pulled the trigger right then, just to see the guy's brains all over the window—until I remembered the car. That is a *great fucking car.* So I stop and make him get out, and I get out the other side. The desert is swirling all around, Sanchez's hair looks like it's going five directions at once, and the guy's just fucking screaming at me—but I can't hear a thing because of the wind even though he's only, what, maybe 10-12 feet away. He starts motioning towards, well *shit,* there wasn't nothing out there, but towards something and gets in my face so I popped him once right in the forehead. I had enough of his fuckin mouth. Even if I couldn't hear him. So the guy goes to his knees. I figure, let the fucker suffer, it's not like he's a saint, y'know? I get in the car and outta fucking nowhere, he's got a *hole* in his head now, the guy attacks the hood of the car. He's bleedin everywhere. So I run him over and double back and with me driving and the wind it's like I'm in a tornado or something—do they have tornadoes in the desert?—anyway, the guy is still not dead! He's on his knees leaning against one arm," Sonny said, and paused there.

"Jesus. So then what?" Harold asked, running his hand over his face.

"So then I got a big start and clipped the fucker at like, 40, or so. Dented my damn fender too. Can't get the spot out, either. And I made way with the cash we was gonna put down for the sale. Anyway, I just wanted to let you know. I felt like I shorted you on the story yesterday. Figured you deserved the whole fuckin weird thing."

"That's a damn strange thing, Son. Kind of a tough guy though, huh?"

"Most Mexicans I met are. Little, but tough as nails, most of em."

"Huh," Harold said. He was still standing in the kitchen doorway. "Much money?" He asked.

"Enough," Sonny answered.

"Yeah."

They each looked about the room, their eyes landing on anything besides one another.

"So back to Central," Sonny said.

"Right. Who you looking for?"

"Billy Banken. Bankley. Ring a bell?"

"Yeah, 'course. Journeyman alto, sits in on some runs, tended bar on a bunch of spots along Central. Never made it, really. Last I saw him he was working Little Harlem for the Brown sisters. It's off Imperial," he said, knowing that Sonny would need more than just a name. After a pause he added, "It's T-Bone Walker's regular gig. The guy's still great."

Sonny looked at the ceiling and said nothing.

"You remember Little Harlem? I took you and Betty there once."

"Can't say that I do, H."

"You got a really bad memory for someone who used to be a dick, you know that?"

"*Was* I a dick?" Sonny asked, and smiled.

"So the guy got *back up* with a bullet in his forehead?" Harold asked, and rubbed his balding head as if the disbelief might be wiped off there.

"Yeah. I couldn't figure it neither."

They each shook their head at the thought.

"You mind if I get comfortable in my own house now? Take my jacket off without people pointing guns at me?" Harold asked. With that he removed his sportcoat and lay it over the chair. Sonny threw him the bottle of whiskey and Harold caught it against his chest and smiled. He went into the refrigerator and bent over and looked at its nearly empty shelves for a long time. Then he closed it without removing anything and he walked to the cabinet and pulled a tumbler and poured himself a drink. "Can I get you anything?" he asked Sonny.

"Actually, I got to get going. Central Avenue calls. And thank you for the *info*, H. Katie calls it *info*, "he said as way of explanation. "And now there's this girl, a deaf Mexican girl at that diner down on Pico"—Sonny looked at H then and stopped speaking. "I dunno. It's all crazy." He tipped his hat and stood. When he reached the back door he turned and asked: "Anything else I need to know before I head down there?"

"Sure. It aint the same no more. It's going to seed. Can't get the big draws now. Lady Day, Duke, the Count, they don't go down there no more. They play in Hollywood now, out west. Bigger money. And you know with Worton running the fuckin department he's still rousting anything walkin' around with a blonde. White or Black. When Parker gets it, it'll be even worse," he said, and looked genuinely sad at the admission.

Sonny nodded.

"But you can still catch Howard Mcghee, Dex Gordon. And T-Bone is still great, man. Catch his act while you can."

"I'll try to notice it."

Harold shook his head. "That won't do," he said. "I want the titles of the first two songs he plays and the last one you see. *Then* I'll know you saw him."

Sonny smiled at Harold's eccentricities and nodded at his old partner. "You got it, H," he said.

11.

Sonny headed south on La Cienega and then east on Slauson, passing invisibly between Century City and Inglewood, crossing Crenshaw and Western and it was not until his ride idled at the signal on San Pedro St that he realized how close he was. The radio was tuned to a country and western station and it played *I'm Movin On* crooned by Hank Snow but Sonny paid no attention to the tune. The mercury drove the night and in it looked so like a shark prowling endlessly. He turned right on Central and there flashing lights along the storefronts and he sat in traffic and there was nothing for it. He parked in an alley behind Club Alabam, whose sign ran vertical and neon red along the avenue. Sonny always parked in alleys. Old habits.

As he sat in the driver's seat, he checked his hat in the rearview mirror. People cared about what they looked like on Central, and if he didn't follow suit, it would bring more attention than his skin already brought. He couldn't do anything about his being white or about the sparrows on his neck or their being seen except wear an ascot—which was something that simply wouldn't happen so long as he was able to dress himself. Besides his neck and hands, he had everything covered, and his sportcoat still fit, albeit snugly, despite the years he had owned it.

He alone walked the alleyway in the near pitchblack night, the muffled lights of two clubs set off to the right as he passed. He hit the mouth of the alley and there turned right and on the corner, Central Ave. It had changed, he was sure, because Harold was seldom mistaken when it came to such things—H cared about this music much more than the police work he was hired to do. But it hadn't changed to Sonny's eyes. Cars double parked in front of clubs like the Jungle Room and the Downbeat, the Plantation Room and Jack's Basket Room, where after hours jams continued still until dawn. Sonny saw negroes young and old in suits and fur felt hats armed with a pride that was often dangerously absent in his run-ins with such people when he was on the force. The cars with which they opened doors for their women read Mercury and Ford and Lincoln and Cadillac. This was their social center, and there was no more happening spot in Los Angeles, despite what the mayor and the map said.

Sonny noticed immediately two black and whites on his block alone, one with its lights blaring. He drew his hat down low about his eyes and footed it south towards Imperial Blvd and the club Harold had called Little Harlem. At the midpoint of the first block, he passed a scene where a cop was frisking a black man pushed against a storefront. The man's blonde date stood on with a look painted on her face that expressed only impossibility. But of course, this was Los Angeles. Sonny figured she could use a trip to Tennessee if she wanted to be shocked.

The man's hat fell off of his head and curled to a finish about his feet. The other cop leaned against the car smoking a cigarette. Sonny noticed the quality of the colored man's coat as he passed. It was a camel hair overcoat, not a fake like his own, double-breasted and with a wide collar. The man's lip was bloody from being smashed against the concrete. Neither officer so much as looked at Sonny and he walked on, not giving another glance to the whole of it.

When he parked, he hadn't realized that the Little Harlem club and Imperial were so far south. He contemplated walking back to his car and driving the distance between them because not having a car available to him quickly limited his options inside the club. If things were to go badly, well, running should be a last option and not the only one, he figured. But he had already walked four blocks. Finally, he reasoned that things would be fine and he cursed his lack of knowledge of the area and his pisspoor memory. He could steal a car if need be, he reasoned.

As he continued walking, the buildings became fewer and there were large lots of kneehigh grass separating them one from another. It felt less controlled and citylike, and Sonny had not seen a black and white for three blocks. He walked on, wondering if soon he would hear the drone of cicadas or the bellow of a lost cow.

And then there it was on the corner. It had only a sign running horizontal above the door and could have otherwise been a drycleaning business or a market. There were sounds coming from within that seemed larger than what the building could accommodate, and several people, all a darker hue than his own, stood outside with drinks in their hands and cigarettes dangling from scissored fingers or closed lips. Sonny walked among them as if he were a regular and lit a cigarette as he approached the door.

"Can I help you?" The man standing at the door who asked that question was staring at Sonny for an answer. Sonny was staring back without one. He figured the man was at least half a foot above six feet and must have weighed 300 lbs. coming out of the womb. He was fat, but even without the fat he was one of the largest men Sonny had ever seen. With it, well, the cake was taken and ran away with and eaten in private.

"Little white man, can I help you?" He tapped Sonny on the shoulder though the bulk of it felt like an anvil.

"I'm just here to see T-bone," Sonny answered.

"You're just here to see T-bone. That right?"

"I heard he's good." Sonny exhaled into the night, craning his neck to shoot the smoke behind him. He hoped the bouncer would take it as a sign of respect.

"He aint jus' good. He's the preeminent bluesman of the West Coast, no doubts or questions aksed." He paused and looked closely at Sonny. "You got a lot of tattoos, man," he said.

It was a statement and not a question. Sonny had nothing for it.

Each stood in the way of the other though the large black man took the entirety of the door frame.

"He on yet?" Sonny asked.

The man looked at the crowd behind Sonny and did not answer. Perhaps there was something more interesting there, or perhaps the man was pretending that there was. Sonny didn't know. Finally, still looking over Sonny's head, he answered: "Yeah. He on. You aint recognized the man's guitar the whole time you been standing here? Get in there and learn yourself somethin."

The bouncer never did look at Sonny as he spoke. He moved aside, which is to say he shuffled sideways to cover only half of the doorway, and Sonny entered.

The main room was dark and nothing special upon first glance. He knew this getup had been around since about 1930 or so, and it didn't seem to have changed much. The stage was set northerly with a large group of round tables, maybe twenty, squatted below and arranged with the performer in mind. There was a small dance floor pulsating with movements Sonny would emulate only when drunk and in front of a mirror. But the patrons here looked good performing them. You certainly wouldn't call them swing dancing, but there was a shared rhythm between the partners that owed an allegiance to it while looking like they were trying to impress one another. Perhaps they were. The bar was built into the wall due south and it barstooled with men in suits and gabardine shirts and women in dresses that hung from their parts like the men wished they could. Though there were some two hundred people here, give or take, by Sonny's count, he was the only white person. Sonny smiled at the whole of it.

The man on stage was chocolate colored and had his hair slicked back and wore a royal blue suit complete with matching shirt and tie. His shoes were a twotone black and white and shone like they were greased. He was playing his guitar behind his head, as was his way given the moment, and he paced about the stage like it had bars he wished to be rid of. Sonny had seen nothing like T-bone Walker. He walked to the bar and stood next to an older man with a closecropped beard. He leaned close to the man and asked: "What's the name of this song?"

The man arched away from him like he was a leper.

"What's this song called?" He shouted again, in the hopes that the man had retreated because he hadn't heard the original question.

"*Bobbysox Blues*, man," the man answered with a tone that suggested that Sonny was perhaps an imbecile for not knowing such a thing.

"Hey thanks," Sonny shouted back. "What was the name of the last one?"

"What?"

"The last song he played, before this one?"

"Hell, I don't know. *Mean old world*, maybe," the man yelled back. It was a conversation in consonant due to the crowd noise that surrounded them. He hoped he would pass Harold's quiz later. "What're you drinkin?" Sonny asked the man.

"Bourbon, son."

Sonny handed the man a dollar, and said, "Buy yourself another. Thanks." With that he walked away. As he sidled along the bar, he grabbed an empty drink not yet disposed of by the bartender. The last remnants of ice slid along the bottom of the highball like they were liquid already. He placed the nearly empty drink on a table which was equally the only one available and the farthest possible location from the stage.

Onstage, T-bone Walker shuffled and shouted and did the splits. He sang the blues and the jump blues and added a bit of swing for good measure. He entertained and catcalled with the crowd. It was clear that this was his house, and he was *the man*. The crowd ate up T-bone, and Sonny could see many of the customers mouthing the words distilled from memory. The dance floor was filled for every song and Sonny looked there, and one lady in particular fastened his eye. She moved like stunted liquid, all waterfall and crashing wave. As if many parts of her shifted in such a way as to have no relation to the rest while containing a graceful unity upon the whole of it.

Sonny sat through two sets in the hopes that the place would thin out but when the band broke off from the stage, the Little Harlem club was more crowded than when he had entered it. He thought of canning the night but knew he didn't have the time. Tomorrow night he would take in the first Hollywood Stars game and shortly thereafter be gone. There would be no more waiting. Four years had been long enough.

T-bone finished his set with a song that Sonny hoped was named *West Side Baby* and walked offstage. Sonny approached the bar. There was an opening at the end of it and he placed his empty glass there and leaned both elbows on the faux marble in the hopes for attention. He tapped his glass three times like he was playing a drumbeat. He tipped back the brim of his hat. He raised his hand. He knocked on the bar like a door. His next trick was going to be stripping naked on the bar for attention but the barkeep made his way over instead.

"What you need, man?" The bartender asked, and as he finished his question, he flipped a towel over his shoulder like every other bartender in every other bar in the world and leaned toward Sonny with a hand at his ear for concentration. He had a wide nose and tight curls along his scalp, and his eyes were set wide and blinked in the darkness. He wore a pencilthin mustache atop his upper lip and when he smiled Sonny noted that one of his incisors was gold. He was a good looking cat, if you leaned that way, but he had the look of a hustler to him and Sonny smelled it.

"I'm lookin for Billy, got a message for him. He around tonight?," Sonny shouted and in the midst of it could hardly hear his own voice.

The man backed off and looked at Sonny anew, as if he needed glasses. "Naw," he answered, "Billy aint been around here for a year or so." He shook his head once and turned and walked briskly away to other duties. Sonny nodded, aware of the fact that he had not been asked again for a drink order.

Sonny called after him but he was gone. Then a man leaned against a mass of people near the center of the bar like they were a cushion against which to galvanize some level of balance. As he forded the space between himself and the bar he yelled, "HEY BILLY, gimme another rum and coke, MAN!" The bartender, the only bartender at present, looked quickly in Sonny's direction and then leaned against the bar and took the empty glass the man handed him.

Sonny looked down and pretended not to have noticed. Because there would be no talking to Billy in here. Not now. Sonny decided quickly to head back to his car and get a bite to eat and wait down the street for Billy's shift to end. He lit a cigarette and set the glass that never belonged to him down on the bar to make for the exit. Before he had really covered any ground at all he found the bouncer standing in his way. He could have been standing anywhere, really, and still been in the way. Sonny looked up at him.

"I was just leaving."

"That's what I hear," the large man said. He had his arms crossed and upon each a slab of muscle that looked cemented. Sonny knew that when those arms unfolded and were used on him it would be painful, regardless of the details. He disliked these moments, the waiting. A piece of him shut down then, an old habit of preparation for events happened upon which the Good Samaritans Club would frown.

"Yeah." Sonny almost smiled, and exhaled this time in the man's face.

"I got a better way, 'less you don't want to co-operate." The man pointed with a finger towards the back door after waving the smoke from his face.

Sonny looked that way and said nothing.

"Let's you and me take a walk," the bouncer said, and when Sonny looked at him the man jutted his chin towards the rear door.

Before Sonny could answer the man was pushing him in that direction like he was Sonny's daddy. Sonny went along like a little boy.

Sonny had not brought his gun that evening from the car. But he knew that this did not call for it now anyway. He slipped both hands into his trouser pockets like he was on an evening stroll and there fastened brass knuckles to the palms of each hand. They fit snuggly onto his thickfingered mitts except for the pinky, each of which felt lost in boundaries too large for their needs. His cigarette dangled pendant from his lips.

The door to the rear of the place was held open by a man roughly the size of the bouncer but without as much menace. Sonny wondered where in the hell they grew them like this. The man in back had replaced girth with fat and muscle with sloppiness though, and was too young to be an expert at anything. Atop his head he wore a hat that may have fit a normal man but looked like a small salesman sample on him and in his left hand he held a baseball bat, the head of which rested on the floor. As Sonny passed him, he removed his right hand from his pocket and in a single fluid motion ripped an uppercut into the man's unprotected and substantial belly. His hand sunk in perhaps six full inches and upon its release the man pouted his lips and let loose a noise not unlike a steam engine coming to a stop, with his hat pitching forward and falling off his head. Sonny heard a "HEY!" from behind him. The sloppy man went to a knee and Sonny quickly wrenched the bat from the man's grip and turned to the monster trailing him. The brass knuckles complicated the grip of the bat but he swung anyway. His father had taught him how to swing a baseball bat a time ago in the confines of Blount County, Tennessee, and he wondered later what his deceased father might think of using such a skill in a vastly different manner from how it was intended. The bouncer had begun a haymaker that may have taken Sonny's head off entire had the bat not simultaneously and sweetly connected with the man's knee, emitting a segmented noise of broken cartilage and hollowsounding bone. The punch hit Sonny square in the left eye and sent him reeling across the alley like he was in a drunken stumble. The bouncer fell like gravity had been increased for him only and held fast to his knee. He gasped in pain and tried to catch his breath like there was not enough oxygen left in Los Angeles. The fatter man was struggling to get up, though it appeared to take some kind of superhuman effort.

Sonny opened his eyes and could see nothing out of the left. He knew that he had been out for a moment because he had no recall of how he had crossed the alley. But there he was, leaning against the concrete wall like it needed his weight to stand. His cigarette was gone. He had dropped the bat on his journey and was wearing only one set of brass knuckles, on his right hand. His hat had sailed off of his head like a flying saucer. He looked quickly for any of those possessions on the ground but saw nothing. He took a moment to assess the situation: the man-mountain was a cripple. He would not be getting up any time soon without some degree of help, and he was squealing but not making too much racket. The other man was to his knees and rising. Sonny moved then without hesitation, closing the width of the alley quickly and leveled two right crosses, steelknuckled, to the head of the man. With the second blow blood shot in linear patterns about the alley as if flicked from the tip of an artist's brush. The man seemed to look once at Sonny with eyes that held no sight in them, and then slumped onto the man beside him, setting off a new wave of piteous groans the added weight had set into motion.

Sonny stood over the two of them and blinked in an attempt to clear his left eye, but there was nothing for it. He could already feel the swelling like tiny balloons injected under the skin there. He touched it once and found blood upon his fingertips. He stepped over the two men and looked into the bar. The rear of the club was some removed from the ballroom, and they had brought him back here for that reason—and for that reason, no one had heard a thing. That would not last long. Sonny had a thought of running into the bar with the bat and taking Billy out with him but a second later found that both unrealistic and possibly insane. He had fucked this up.

He hopped over the two bodies, one writhing slowly and the other not moving at all, and walked the alley looking for the bat or his knuckles. He never did find his knuckles, but the bat had skittered some twenty feet north. His hat was not far from it. He picked the bat up and rehatted himself and looked back once at the exit and footed his way north without another thought. In the alley a block up he found one of the large deserted lots which he had passed on the street just two hours earlier, and here he tossed the bat into the weeds. He found then that he was still wearing his brass knuckles, tainted a shiny crimson in the starlight. He wiped them on the long grass and pocketed them and continued north, noting that one of his sportcoat pockets had ripped off. He wondered when that had happened.

Two blocks further he was beginning to get a grasp of the situation. He had to get to his car, and he had to cross the street and two alleys to do it. He could not risk being stopped by a black and white for any reason whatever. That would be bloody, and he would be on the losing end of it as night closed regardless. He wondered, and not for the first time, why he was dumb enough to park so far away.

The alleys at this time of night were busy with shadows. Sonny stayed in the center of the alley, lamplit, stumbling his way about in the hopes of being mistaken for a slightly tipsy man struggling to find his bearings. He passed three men passing for thugs and smoking cigarettes.

Two of them glared hard at Sonny but he let it go. This was no time for theatrics. Towards the end of that block he leaned against a car momentarily. In the halflight it looked like a baby blue Ford, with chrome lines and whitewalls. It was a nice ride. He kept hearing little noises, like faroff grunts and squeaks that he could not place. He turned his head to the sound, and finally assumed that it was his head. It would not be the first time that he was making things up, though it might be the first time sober. It was then he felt the car shift under him and saw two black faces with naked torsos, one of which held a large rack of breasts, staring out at him from windows slightly steamed over and opaque. The man wiped his sweaty forehead and then ran his bare arm in a circle and all four eyes, one man and one woman, looked at him like the outside was a different world entire. They seemed out of breath. He raised a hand as a gesture of hello and smiled, bringing his face in full view. The woman gasped and backed away into the darkness. The man wore an expression that had once been shock but had morphed into anger and Sonny tapped the car with his finger twice and started walking. He considered what his eye must look like for people to be gasping at the site of him. It felt about the size of an apple. Maybe that's what's growing up there, he thought.

When Sonny had covered perhaps fifty feet he heard a car door open behind him and there the man from the car in various degrees of undress according to location. He had one foot out the door and was shaking his fist at Sonny, shouting, "Come back here, you muthafucka! What the *fuck* you think you're *doin?*" Sonny moved out of the lamplight and into the darkness of back doors of various bars and clubs and shops closed for the night. He hoped the man wouldn't follow. He wasn't sure he could afford another skirmish tonight, being a weeknight and all. He walked on.

On the last block before he had to cross Central Ave and get to his car, his foot struck something in the darkness and sent him pitching forward, almost falling. There was a grunt accompanied with the action which he assumed to be his own. He walked back to see what had caused his clumsiness and as the gradations of darkness grew to various levels of charcoal and grey he made out a leg, and then a foot. A man was sitting against the back wall of a barber shop. There would be no reason for any well person to be doing such a thing, so Sonny kicked the leg and turned to go. It was then that a hand grabbed Sonny's trouser leg. Sonny turned quickly and with his right hand pummeled the man in darkness, twice. Neither blow connected solidly but both were sent forth with enough meaning to make a point nonetheless. The man gurgled, groaned, and spat. Sonny knelt down and saw then that the man was far worse off than he had initially guessed. Against his better judgment, or any judgment at all, Sonny sat down to get a closer look at the man. It was a painful process, sitting. Don't try it at home. So full of starts and stops and ending with an exhalation of breath Sonny didn't realize he was carrying with him. He couldn't remember when a single punch from any man, even the world's largest man, had carried with it such exhaustion. He wondered if Little Harlem would be sending out a posse after him. And here he was, sitting in an alley with some jack who couldn't stand if Lana Turner needed help with her bathrobe. Maybe he was just getting old, he thought absently.

The man leaning against the barber shop looked at Sonny with eyes that held no light in them whatever. He was young, perhaps twenty-five, and lightskinned. He smiled, actually it was a grimace, but it was as close as he could come to smiling at present. The incisor on his right side glinted gold in the Los Angeles night.

"Too drunk, buddy?"

The man laughed then, or tried to, though it looked more painful that anything Sonny had ever done. It was full of wheezing and gurgling.

"Alright," Sonny said, as way of excusing himself, and began the process of standing again.

"No, *please*," the man wheezed. It sounded like a desperate whisper, one spoken for necessity rather than affect. "I need—." He stopped there, and continued breathing with what sounded like a child's rattle in his chest.

"Look, I got problems too, man," Sonny said. "I got to get out of here. I don't have time for this shit. I got King Kong chasing me a couple blocks back."

The man looked up at him then, and Sonny saw a desperation he recognized in the faces of victims. A few had been his own. Most had belonged to people who realized the stakes in the game long after the bet had officially been placed. It was something that could not be faked.

"This is my key," the man said. In his hand, he held a key that hung pendant on a homemade necklace of leather. He placed it with some effort near Sonny's hand. It had a piece of plastic connected to it but it was far too dark to read what it contained on it. Sonny recognized the shape of the plastic as belonging to a motel.

"You okay, man? I don't want your key," Sonny said, and looked up and down the dark alley, which seemed as dark and as empty at when he had entered it.

"Please. I'm dyin, man. I mean—," he stopped and wheezed.

Sonny leaned forward and touched the belly of the man. It was soaked in a thick liquid he could not mistake after all these years. There was a piece of the man that belonged inside of him that lay outside as if it were just taking a peek at what it had missed all these years. Sonny took a closer look then and the puddle the man sat in was blood as well. Sonny shook his hand loose and looked at the man.

"What the fuck?"

"I been gutted, man. Like a dog. Fuck. I'm scared, man, I got pins and needles all up in my legs. Take my key, please," he said, and stopped to catch his shortening breath. He had tears streaming down both cheeks. The end was near, and Sonny recognized it like a confession he wanted no part of. Truth or no truth.

"No, kiddo. I mean, I'll get you some help," he said. Sonny placed his hand on the young man's forehead and it was ice cold, colder than Sonny ever wanted to be.

The man exhaled in pieces.

"This is my key." He paused. "To my hotel room." Another pause. "I got money. And stuff. In a bag." He stopped then. Sonny wondered if he would speak again.

He slapped him softly on the cheek.

The man woke then, as if from a short nap. "Take it, please," the man pleaded. "Please. To my wife, my son." He inhaled twice, two big gulps for air that ended as if there were none. "Tell my wife I love her. Tell..." One deep wheeze. "My son I'm proud. Say sorry. Sorry. So so Sorry." He swung his hand with the key towards the body of Sonny, a gesture as blind as it was desperate. His breathing was shallow and quick. Shallow and slow. Then none at all.

Sonny slapped the man once, twice, but he was gone.

"Fuck. Fuck, fuck, *fucker*," Sonny said, and stood. "Fuck!"

He looked up into the night sky and the small constellation of stars visible that night. He could see the palm trees lined like soldiers in some silent march descend in the bottom of his vision west to east, the fronds rustling softly in the faint breeze. As if there were answers attainable and worth the trouble up there in that bowl of stars. Some level of balance where evil and good alike walked a land so barren that the giving and taking of life were concepts upon which the stars broke themselves. The place where everybody pays.

"*Fuck*," he repeated. Like he was playing with a word he had just learned. He nearly dropped the key onto the body of the boy, and he wanted to, but something stopped him. Some level of decency that he assumed had been beaten from him in the war, taken from him as a cop, voided altogether in Mexico. But here it was, hanging onto these keys like it knew the kid.

He walked towards the center of the alley and its dim stream of light. He held the key up and the plastic piece connected said Property of the Aces High Motel. The number on the key was 4. Sonny sighed and put the key into his trouser pocket. He footed it north again and crunched his hat low and turned west at the end of the alley. Upon reaching the end of the block the arrow turned green and without breaking stride he walked into the street and across Central Ave. He kept his eyes below his brim and his face aimed squarely at the sidewalk in front of him. Had Central been having a fullscale riot, Sonny would not have noticed a thing. He reached the sidewalk and continued walking.

His Merc was still in the alley. Its absence was a possible difficulty he had not really wanted to address, and he was relieved that he didn't need to. The engine purred and snapped at the night. He revved the engine twice and glided south out of the alley towards the Little Harlem club. The entrance was not as peopled as when he had arrived and he saw no sign of the bouncer. But then, he thought, the bouncer can't stand up anymore, so of course I don't see him. He sat at the corner and idled, the heavythroated growl of the engine pitching exhaust skyward. He lit a cigarette and fingered the .45 in his lap. He didn't see bartender Billy. He would return tomorrow, he thought, and gunned the engine, turned and headed west.

***

Some ten minutes later he exited the car and left it idling at the curb while he picked up a pay phone receiver and dialed the operator.

"How may I help you?"

"Tell the fuzz there's a corpse in the eastern alley across the street from Club Alabam on Central."

"Tell the—? Sir, I'm afraid—"

"I'm hanging up. Tell them, the alley across the street from Club Alabam."

"Sir, I don't—"

Sonny hung up and thumbed through the yellow pages also in the phone booth. Such efficient things, little worlds all to themselves, those booths. He found the Aces High Motel on Culver Blvd and set to memorizing the address. He exited the booth and sat in the Mercury. The traffic was light. It was late. The cops would find the body of the kid and eventually locate where he had been staying. Maybe tonight. Probably not. But either way Sonny had to get to the Aces High and get the kid's crap out so he could take it to his wife and son. It was the least he could do. He owed the kid that much, didn't he?

12.

The Aces High motel was clearly not inhabited by people who were accustomed to that hand. Nor was it in an area that would be included in the tourist pamphlets for Culver City, though Sonny had slept in worse. It squatted in the middle of National Blvd a mere five blocks east from Harold's apartment complex, though a jarring five blocks at that. Sonny cruised by the entrance slowly and found only two cars in the given parking spaces. Not nearly enough traffic for him to be discreet. The neon sign outside was missing two letters and you couldn't tell what suite the cards were. Sonny doubted that the occupants here cared much. He traveled west to the end of the block and parked there, grabbed a flashlight he had in the trunk, and walked north to the alley and back east again. The intent was to find an entrance through the alley and enter the kid's room undetected. Either that, or he simply loved parking blocks away from where his intentions lay—and Los Angeles has wonderful alleys, wide and lighted. Don't let anyone tell you different.

Upon reaching the halfway point in the block, Sonny recognized the back of the motel. There was a small entrance into the courtyard from the alley and he took it. The trash dumpster was positioned there and gave the evening a new aroma. With the number 4 Sonny assumed that the room would be on the first floor rather than the second, and upon entering the courtyard he was proved correct. There were still the same two cars parked, though now the overwhelming smell of marijuana hung about the place like a skunky incense. The office was located in the front of the driveway though it was dark and appeared it would remain so. Room 4 was the second room from the corner, five rooms on each floor, ten total. There were overhead hall lights but the janitor must have been the one smoking the reefer because not many worked. There was a man slumped into himself leaning against room 5, and Sonny had to step over him to get to the kid's room. The man was either asleep or dead, Sonny couldn't tell and wasn't interested besides.

The insertion of the key into the lock and the opening of the door was incalculably loud given the emptiness of the place. Sonny grimaced as if that might lessen the noise and was as careful as he could manage and still created enough racket to nearly wake the guy leaning on room 5, who may have been dead. He closed the door behind him and nobody ever tried harder to keep a door quiet. He left it a hairline fracture open to avoid the noise of the lock and further racket.

Once inside, he flipped on the flashlight. From what Sonny could tell, it looked like a hotel room. Greens and browns and not one thing you would ever want in your home. The mattress was a substitute for concrete. The chair had a rip in the backrest and the cushion couldn't really be called one. He saw no bags, no sign that anyone at all had stayed here. Walking past the bed, he found the closet empty. Two hangers doing exactly that. The bathroom was likewise empty. The drains were brown and the towel hung in folds. Sonny turned around and decided to fine comb the place because this scene didn't make sense, and it was then he saw in the smallish circle of light what he had missed the first time. The erect handle of a suitcase jutting out an inch from underneath the bed. He kneeled down and pulled out a horizontally placed leather satchel with a widemouth opening and a strap across the zipper, in the style of a large doctor's bag. He placed that on the bed and looked underneath the frame, in the chest of drawers, in the nightstand. All empty. The kid wasn't exactly cozy here.

Sonny sat down on the bed and picked up the luggage. He considered rifling through it here but saw no point. In his own hotel room he would take his time. Nothing was going anywhere. He stood to go with the bag in one hand and the flashlight in the other as the door to the room swung open. A man stood in the doorway, though at present he was only a backlit silhouette. It was a silhouette of broad shoulders and a small waist, hatless, with the rounded physique that suggested a musculature without detail.

"What you doin in here?" the voice asked. It was a deep voice that seemed unconvinced of its toughness.

"Out for a midnight stroll. Figured I'd lift a bag or two. You know how it is," Sonny answered.

"You aint leavin here 'less I know who you are and why you're here."

Neither man said anything then and instead stared at the lack of detail of one another.

"Look, pal. You the manager?" Sonny asked.

"You LAPD?"

Sonny thought about that one. The opening was there, but he couldn't allow himself the pleasure. Then: "I'm somebody you don't want to mess with, son."

"Then let's just say I'm a concerned citizen."

Sonny flipped the flashlight into the man's face, who recoiled for a second, then leaned in the door frame and turned on the overhead lights.

"What'd you do that for? The flashlight was my ace in the hole," Sonny said.

The man wore an A shirt and a pair of pleated trousers and was perhaps mulatto. His hair curled tightly to his head and he wore a broad nose, but his skin color was nearly olive. His eyes were green. He had no shoes on. He looked to Sonny like he carried the intelligence and attitude of a primal beast, but mistakes were without handle now.

"That's a helluva shiner you got there, man," the stranger said.

"Yeah. It's my second head. He's glad to meet you."

The man took a step toward Sonny, who looked him over closely.

"Look, tough guy. Do you have a weapon here?" Sonny asked, "Cause I don't see one. And unless you've got some steel on you this conversation is a waste of my time."

"Put the bag down," the man said. "That's Hank's bag. He been staying here," the man said, in the most rational tone possible.

"Doesn't look like it," Sonny said, and let his eyes wander about the newly lit room. "Look," he continued, "this is gonna go badly for you unless you move. I won't say it again."

"I can't let you take my friend's bag," the man said, in a tone that that lacked both conviction and reason.

Sonny placed the flashlight on the bed with care and removed the .45 from his waistband and casually swung it until it the barrel was a single eye trained on the man, who put his hands up in recognition that the situation had developed into a hand more than he was willing to play.

"Don't shoot me, man. I'm just tryin to help a guy out."

"Yes. I'm sure the part of good Samaritan and you are well acquainted. Or, umm, maybe just trying to help yourself out. Turn the lights off."

"Please, man. He was begging now." The transition had come quickly. "Don't—"

"*Turn the lights out.* If you don't do it soon, I will shoot you and leave you in that ridiculous chair. You will die there. Is that what you want?" Sonny asked.

The man stood and shuffled over to the wall, keeping his eyes on the gun the whole time, and ran his fingers along the wall. He missed the switch twice, but hit it on the third try.

"Now look outside and make sure that no one sees us. If you try to run, I will shoot you in the back. Happily."

The man reluctantly turned his head from the gun and swiveled it in the hallway.

"Nobody there, man. 'Cept that dude in the hall."

"Now shut the door and sit back down," Sonny said.

He did.

"Thanks for your cooperation. Now these are your choices: 1. I can shoot you, which we've already gone over, 2. You can answer any and all questions I ask you about Hank, or 3. Well—there isn't really a three. But three choices always sounds better—I imagine you'd like a three."

"Whatever you need, man. I'll answer whatever you need." The man answered frantically, sensing an opportunity he did not know existed just seconds before.

"First, what's your name?"

"Howard. Howard Wilson," he said. He put his hands up and softly slapped them down on his knees as if some exclamation writ there.

"How do you know Hank?"

"Awww, man. I just met the cat last week. He just got out the joint."

"Why was he here?"

"I dunno, man. I mean, how am I s'posed to know? He said he had some business. I don't aks questions like that. Not around here. Everybody got some story. You know how that shit go."

Sonny digested this and was silent for a moment.

"Hank is dead," Sonny said, finally. "I didn't kill him. If I had, I would tell you, and then kill I would kill you too. But I just found him with his guts hangin all over him in an alley somewhere. He told me to see his wife and son about something. He tell you about them?"

Howard exhaled at this information and ran his hands along his thighs, thinking. Finally, realizing that a question had been asked of him:

"Just that he had 'em. Said he was goin' down to see 'em when he was done here."

"You said *down.* Going down where?"

"New Orleans, I think. He had a accent like any other backwoods southern nigga," the man said. Sonny saw him eye the suitcase hungrily. "What you think in there?" He asked, and nodded towards it with his chin.

Sonny smiled at Howard. "I think that it aint your business. I think that you should keep thoughts like the one you just had out of your head," Sonny said, and stood, gun extended.

"I mean, aint you even curious?"

"Not here I'm not. What do you think? Guy just gets out of the joint, if that's straight, he comes here for business? Must be business he had to finish from before he was in the joint. So he either comes here for money owed him or to square a beef. Use your head. Either way, he fucked up 'cause I'm betting right now all he really wanted was to go home to his wife and kid, and trust me when I tell you that I'm a pisspoor substitute for a homecoming."

The mulatto man said nothing in return, but nodded, and continued nodding, as he rubbed his thighs.

"I'm gonna leave now. I'm taking the case," Sonny said, deliberately. "Just sit there and watch me and you'll see tomorrow.

Sonny took a step with the bag towards the door and Howard made his move. He was too hungry not to. He grabbed the lamp on the table in an attempt to throw it at Sonny. The motel lamp didn't move, however, because it was bolted to the table. Upon realizing this Howard frantically grabbed at the sides of the table but could not wield its awkward girth. He looked at Sonny then, his face filled with panic.

"Unfuckingbelievable," Sonny said, and shot Howard once in the forehead, a single dimesize hole that created a much larger one upon exiting the rear of the brainpan. A fan of crimson covered the walls of the back corner and side curtain. Howard stood a moment and bobbed like a felled boxer before he collapsed onto the unwieldy table and rolled off that onto the floor, dead as dead gets.

Sonny put the gun into his waistband and quickly removed the man's shirt and wrapped it awkwardly around what remained of his head and grabbed Howard by the armpits and dragged him into the hallway and over the legs of the man leaning against door 5 and into the small entryway leading to the alley. With no small effort he raised the man and awkwardly rolled him into the dumpster one body part at a time. He heard the body finally collapse against the assorted trashbags and then silence. He hurried back to the room and the bag there on the bed. He took a handkerchief out of his back pocket and wiped down the doorknobs and dresser handles. Sonny picked up the flashlight and bag and closed the door behind him with the handkerchief. As he footed the hallway he leaned next to the man lying near door 5. Still nothing. He couldn't hear breathing and it was too dark to see. He was still either dead or asleep. Sonny walked into the alley and stayed tight to the left side and the folds of darkness there. He wanted a cigarette desperately but did not fumble for one.

Upon reaching his car, Sonny opened his trunk and placed the bag and the flashlight on the floor of it. He closed his trunk. Sat in his car. Started the engine. When he revved the motor, a guttural howl into the night, he screamed "ARE YOU FUCKING KIDDING ME! Is this a fucking game! What the *fuck*!!" He slumped his head onto his steering wheel and winced like the gods had deserted him when the left side of his head touched it. When he raised his head he looked skyward but was talking to the dead kid: "You better be worth it, you asshole. *Fuckin New Orleans??*" The words hung in the car and did not dissipate as he traveled east, towards his own couch for the night, as the early morning darkness draped the city streets and the storied Los Angeles of tabloids and film reels hid behind iron gates.

***

Sonny did not park in the parking lot but instead on Grand St in front of the Elmwood Arms Hotel. He looked at the building a moment before he exited the car, amazed at how comforting it looked compared to the Aces High. The contrast therein. Which was really saying something. Like the contrast from rancid pork to Spam.

The lobby was empty, of course. The hotel lobby that finds itself crowded at half past one in the morning is either a terrible place to be or too expensive to think about, and the Elmwood Arms was neither. The rug was still dirty and the gum stains had not moved. The worn couches and chairs were sleeping. The man behind the counter was not, however, as he was shuffling papers. Every clerk in every hotel from here to Nova Scotia shuffles papers whenever they get the chance. Just like every bartender throws his towel over his shoulder and wipes down glasses all day long, every day. He was the same gent who had checked Sonny in, and his foppish brown hair parted on the left and slicked down. He smiled when he saw Sonny approach, but it was a smile without any humanity to it.

"And how has your stay been thus far, sir?"

Sonny looked at the man and stopped walking some six feet from the counter. He did not respond.

The concierge barreled forward: "I certainly hope you didn't acquire that terrible knot on your eye on *our* premises," he said.

"I don't know what you're talking about," Sonny answered.

"Your eye, sir. It's purple and blue and three times the size of the other. Surely you—"

Sonny smiled and looked down at his ripped sportcoat and soiled pants. The leather satchel he held. Then he pointed to his eye as if he had never thought of it prior. "Oh, *that*," he said. "Yeah. Well, it's a story. And see, the thing is, I'm just not interested in sharing."

The clerk shuffled something in front of him.

"It's alright, sweetcakes," Sonny amended. "Some rough love is all. But the room has been swell so far. Honestly."

"The girl you have staying with you seems nice."

"She's a sweetheart. She's perfect. Remember that, and then don't ever mention her again," Sonny said. He fingered a Chesterfield from his pack and stuck it between his lips and lit the thing.

"Yes, sir," the concierge said. "What did you say your name was, sir?"

"I haven't yet," Sonny answered, and exhaled.

"Yes. Well then. I will be needing those registration papers from you shortly."

"Sure. Shortly it is." Sonny smiled with the cigarette between his lips. "Hey, Chuck around?"

"No sir. Charles has the evening, er, morning off."

"Good. He's a good kid. I hope he fails miserably in Hollywood but makes it another way. Failing in this fuckin town is a credit to your personality anyway." He paused, and added, "But don't tell him I said that."

"What do you mean, sir?" The clerk looked surprised in the way that bad actors act surprised.

"You figure it out. I'm going to bed. Anybody in the elevator?"

"We are between men right now, besides Charles. But I would be happy to find some—"

Sonny waved off the suggestion before he had even heard it. "Don't bother," he said. "I got a head full of questions anyway. I can probably get em all answered in the time I'm on that thing."

The man looked to speak again and then nodded and Sonny walked towards the stairwell carrying the leather bag, the unlit cigarette still hanging pendant from his lips.

***

Sonny sat on his couch that morning and placed the satchel on the table in front of him. He reached to open it but did not. He stared at it, as if perhaps it might join the silent conversation. Then he stood, walked into the bedroom and there in the doorframe witnessed Katie sleeping for the second time since his return, her head at peace against the give of a pillow, her freckles evident even in the halflight. Sonny missed his wife and what she would say about moments like this. Sonny had no words for them thus making memory elusive at times. There were images, but no symphony to accompany them. Betty had a way of phrasing the present in such a way as to ensure its immortality. He chalked that up as another thing he missed on what had become an endless list and closed the door to the bedroom and sat back heavily on the couch.

He leaned over and turned on the lamp and then clicked open the strap on the bag, unzipping the main section. He grabbed the two handles and pulled the wide mouth open. Tightly shrinkwrapped stacks of cash sat atop whatever bounty lay beneath. There were four of them. Three stacks of twenty-dollar bills and one stack contained one hundred dollar bills, if one could measure the inside by the outside contents. Sonny placed those on the couch. Underneath those were two A-shirts and a pair of pants, folded according to the pleats. One pair of black socks. A razor, and a toothbrush. No booze. Sonny kept all of these in their given position and placed them on the couch. On the bottom of the bag lay assorted photographs and letters addressed to one Hank Fontenot at Alcatraz Island State Prison, San Francisco, Ca. Sonny picked up a handful and placed them on his lap. Most of the letters were typewritten, meaning that they had been rewritten by the guards after they had been received. Sonny

knew that to be a policy up there because it was considered a Limited

Privilege prison. He and Harold had discussed the difficulties of the policy

as some of the myths filtered their way through the police ranks. He knew

Machine Gun Kelly and Capone had both done jolts there. He looked

down again. A few of the letters were in a woman's script, one full of

loops in a delicate hand and decorated with hearts. Some of the sentences

had been blacked out. Sonny thought of the favors Hank must have owed

the guards to receive the actual letters. Good for him, he thought. Sonny

figured it must have been worth the debt regardless.

He looked closely at one of the handwritten letters and read:

Dearest Hank-

I can't imagine what horrors they must be putting you through in that

horrible place. Please know that Theodore and I miss you more each day

you are gone. Stay strong, my love, and know that as absence makes the

heart grow fonder, I do believe mine is set to burst. I am so sorry I am

unable to visit because of the money we talked about, but I pray each and

every night for your parole hereing in just six months. Six months, after all

we have been through. I believe in it this time, honey. I just know that

you'll make them let you go.

Rhonda has made arrangements for Theo to go to a private school

next fall. I had been—

Sonny stopped there. He felt like he was listening to a conversation he had no business in. But of course he did, right? The letter was signed Etta and dated September of 1949. Taking the six months from there, he must have made parole. So why come down to Los Angeles when your wife and boy, still waiting for you, were in New Orleans? Sonny wanted the answer, but figured he already knew. And he had other business to attend here. One big, fat, greasy reason wearing a suit and stained shirts. Just thinking of the greaseball and what he had done to his life brought with it an anger that sat in Sonny's throat like bile.

He put the letters down and picked up some photographs. They were black and white and sepia-toned. They portrayed a prettyish young lightskinned negro woman in many of them. In two of them in particular, she was standing in a flowered sundress next to her boy who had reached that awkward and gangly age of perhaps eight. His knees and feet looked too large for a man twice his size, yet his body had the linear verticality of youth. He was of a darker hue than his mother. Etta and Theodore.

Sonny leaned back on the couch with the letters and photos splayed about him and soon fell asleep with the photo of mother and child pressed lightly against his breast as if their love for a fallen husband could find a kinship with his own affection for what was lost. As if second chances could find some redemption, some rebirth, even vicariously, in the dimestore love affair of a con and the family he left behind.

13.

Sonny woke to Katie standing over him and his collection of memorabilia. He initially didn't know where he was or what the papers around him were. His head felt stretched and heavy. He couldn't immediately see out of his left eye. Katie had one of the letters in her hand.

"Mornin, Sonny. It's almost 11. I figured—"

"You figured right. Thanks." Sonny rubbed the back of his head and rested his hand on the base of his neck as he sat up.

Katie was wearing a fitted black dress with a sailor's collar and fishnet stockings. The dress was old and bit worn at the edges which did nothing to take away from its appeal. The skeleton still hung between her collarbones. Her eyes were shadowed and she wore a red flower in her hair. She wore no lipstick, but didn't need any. Sonny kicked himself for his age and his relationship to her and those thoughts without handle.

"You look gorgeous, honey. What for?"

She sat on the couch with a bounce and smiled at him: "Sometimes a girl just needs to look nice," she answered.

"Well, you succeeded like an H-bomb."

She blushed and bit her lower lip and looked down. Then she leaned towards him and put a weightless finger against his purple and swollen eye. Even that hurt. "That looks—gosh," she said. "That must really sting."

Sonny smiled. "Yeah, it *really* does," he admitted.

"How'd you get it? Is that an okay question?"

"Of course it's an okay question, doll. I'm looking for a guy that'll help me with Betty's death. He didn't want to talk to me."

"That guy Billy whoever?"

"Just a guy, Katie." He smiled at her then, and said, "He'll see the light, eventually."

Katie said nothing but leaned her head against his shoulder. It was an action so honest and unfailingly graceful that Sonny didn't bother to move her. They stayed like that as if they belonged there, leaning against one another.

"I'm going to the Stars game tonight. Wanna come?" Sonny asked, while staring out into the late morning beyond the sliding glass door. The question surprised even him. He didn't know it was there. It hadn't been there moments before.

Her eyes lit at the suggestion. "Of course!" She said, and sat up on the couch.

"Okay. I got some business to take care of though. So you need to promise to stay out of the way when I need you to. Got it?"

She saluted him, still smiling. "Hey," she said, "I meant to ask you. What does that lettering on the outside of your forearm mean?"

Sonny looked at it as if he had not been aware of it before. Between a pair of nautical stars were the words *Hold Fast*. He smirked at her. "It means 'hang in there.' It's an old sailor's term for holding onto the rigging during storms so they wouldn't be tossed overboard. For me, it means hang in there—even when maybe you shouldn't. Get it?"

She nodded. "Okay," she said. "I saw that on a guy's knuckles one time, in a club on Sunset. I took him, after a while. But he was good. Real good. And Mick was with me then. I think I needed him to be." She looked almost uncomfortable at the admission.

Sonny grimaced at the memory though he had no part in it.

"So, what are these letters and pictures about?" She asked, and ran her arm in an arc over the whole of them.

"A guy I met last night. He needs some help."

"He gave you these?"

Sonny looked down and wondered at how he should explain it. He decided that he hadn't decided yet. "I'll tell you what," he said. "Tonight when I pick you up, at six, out front, I'll give ya the whole dirty deal. It's a long story. Have your bags packed." He pointed at her before he continued. "Six, no later." He repeated the instructions because he needed to hear them and he needed to be sure that she was hearing them.

She looked at him, obviously disappointed about not getting the full story. And then it was gone. In an instant. "I gotta go," she said. "I'm helping Mick out with something. That's why the getup. He told me not to tell you. But oh well." She shrugged her shoulders at her lack of willpower and felt no less for it.

Sonny looked at her with what he hoped would look like concern.

"It's *fine*, Sonny. It's just a meeting with this guy he's trying to get to finance something. He's gonna set a game up." She leaned down like somebody twice her age and rubbed the underside of her hand over his cheekbone. She watched her mama too much, Sonny thought, and nobody ever tried harder not to show it.

"Six o'clock then. Out front," he said.

"Got it, Sarge."

"If you've got bags, have em with you. Just in case," he repeated again.

She looked at nothing certain and then nodded, once.

"You okay with this? I can leave you here," he said. "I mean, where I'm going I'm not even sure—"

She nodded again and said: "I'm sure. I'll be ready," and then she smiled at Sonny and grabbed her clutch and walked out the door. She turned before it closed and blew a kiss to him. Sonny cursed himself after she left and walked to the bathroom with his .45 and took an icecold shower that had it been in an igloo could not have been cold enough.

Sonny dressed in his white collared shirt and pleatless chinos. He slicked his hair back and rolled his sleeves to his elbows. He touched the knotted bulb that had taken over his left eye socket and marveled at the purple stain rimmed in yellow it had become. The eyeball itself was stained red and contained within it circuitous knots of a red webbing scattershot in every direction. There was a knock on the door and Sonny picked the .45 off the bed and cracked it. It was Chuck, as expected, with the coffee Sonny had requested.

Sonny quickly stuffed the gun in the rear of his pants and took the coffee from Chuck's outstretched arm.

"Thanks, kiddo."

"No problem, Mr. Sonny."

"Not Mr. Sonny, just Sonny."

"Yessir."

"Okay. When I ring the elevator in a few minutes I might need help taking some things to the car."

"Of course," the kid said. He smiled the smile that would always make him the recipient of kindness without regard to what is deserved. Then the boy turned and walked away.

Sonny closed the door and sipped the coffee. It was still steaming and quite bitter. The glass door to the deck was open and the day was heating up, the Santa Ana's riding the backbone of the San Gabriel and Santa Monica mountain ranges like a madness loosed upon the sane. Dry enough to spit cotton, Sonny's daddy would've said. He smiled at the thought.

He walked back into the bedroom and looked upon the bed where the odds and ends of his scavenged collection of articles lay. Hank's refilled and zippered leather bag. Shiv's snubnose revolver, loaded now with the five bullets Sonny found in the glove box. His own .45, fully loaded and with an extra magazine next to it. His one remaining set of brass knuckles. His suitcase. His overcoat. Both hats. An ankle holster he had taken off a cuff years ago. He attached it and inserted Shiv's snubnose. The gun within was loose and would rattle a bit and act as an annoyance when he walked, but it would hold. He put the knuckles in his pocket. Then he opened his suitcase and off the top took a stack of bills. It had been fortunate for him that the deal he had falsely negotiated with Sanchez had been in American dollars. Getting that amount of pesos changed over would have been difficult, but that reason alone was why the previous three payments he had arranged had been in dollars. He took three bills off the top and tied the stack with a rubber band and placed it back in the case. He dropped the .45 in the pocket of the overcoat. He had earlier decided that he would stow all of his belongings in the car in the off chance that tonight did not go well.

Then he sat on the bed, sipped his coffee, and thought. Why was he bringing Katie to the game tonight? Because if he had to run, he needed her with him, that was one answer. Was that it? And once he confronted Vinny tonight, who was sure to be at the game with Mickey, his face and name would be all over the streets. Mickey had powerful connections in the department, and he would put them to use. Everything would speed up exponentially tonight. That was why he needed Katie with him. But could he ensure her safety? He pushed that thought away like it hadn't been there to begin with. And from here? New Orleans? He had never been to New Orleans, but he had heard stories from his father. He shook his head at the uncertainty of the whole of it, but it was barreling towards him nevertheless. That much he knew. And the fact of the matter was that he had made the choice to return to Los Angeles a wanted man in the hopes of making one man pay for his wife's murder. That hadn't changed. He would start with Billy and end it, he hoped, with Vinnie. Sonny went down the stairwell and moved the Mercury to the underground lot to avoid being seen carrying his baggage through the lobby. Call him paranoid.

He stood in the hallway with his bags and accessories littering the carpet. He rang the elevator. Sometime later that afternoon it arrived. Chuck helped Sonny load the elevator, and they began the trip to the parking garage.

"Are you leaving us?" Chuck asked.

Sonny raised his eyebrows and looked at Chuck. He exhaled deeply. "You're nosy, kid. Don't let it getcha in trouble."

"I'm sorry. I just—I mean, your bags."

They both looked down at the bags. They weren't moving themselves.

"I just figured," he said, and shrugged.

"Not sure yet," Sonny began. "But I may be leaving the elegant confines of the Elmwood Arms tonight. We'll see." He winked at Chuck.

"Good luck then. I mean, you know, if you *do* go."

"Thanks. You too, kid. "

"If you don't mind me asking, did you get hit there? In your eye?" He pointed to the eye as he asked the question, in case there was any confusion.

"No, Chuck. I just wake up this way sometimes. Makes the day more interesting," Sonny answered.

They both looked up at the numbers. They were nearing 3. It's difficult to say a proper goodbye when time is suspended.

Chuck shuffled his feet and looked down.

"What is it, kid?"

He looked up and his cheeks were blushed. "Well, uhhhhhh," he stammered. "I was wondering if the girl you had with you, I mean, I was wondering if she would be going— with you."

Sonny looked at him and said nothing.

Chuck looked down again. Shameful without reason.

"Yeah, she's going with me, Chuck. But she may be back later on today if you want another look. And you're a good kid. So let's us leave her outta this."

"Yessir. Anthony asked me to remind you about the paperwork, sir."

Sonny smiled for the first time that morning. "Is that the fop's name, Anthony?"

"What's a fop, sir?"

"It's what Anthony is. Never mind. Tell him that it's on its way," he said, and then softly hit Chuck on the shoulder. "But just between you and me, it aint on the way," he said.

"Right," Chuck said. The young man smiled uneasily.

The elevator came to a stop in the garage. Chuck helped Sonny carry everything out and placed it in the trunk of the car. Twice Sonny saw Chuck look at the back of his pants as he bent over and knew that he was looking at the bulge of the gun there. Or, he hoped he was. Finally Sonny walked to the driver's side door and opened it. He called Chuck over and extended his hand, inside of which was a folded and crisp bill it would take Chuck weeks at his current position to earn. They shook. Chuck walked away and soon found himself in the elevator looking out at Sonny and waiting for the doors to close. He waved at Sonny who nodded but did not wave back.

Sonny started the engine to the Mercury and let it idle. It sounded like it was the one with the smoking problem. It chortled and coughed and finally found a rhythm and then hummed like the song had only one note. Sonny let it run its course. He had plenty to think about. He wondered at the ridiculousness of his actions here and the futility of revenge and its dangers. He might not make the evening, and therein lay the challenge to the thing. He couldn't very well die in front of Katie. That would be embarrassing and ridiculous and no way to end his given time on this rock. Perhaps that was why he was bringing her along, he thought. He shook his head at the possibilities of the day.

A TRUNK FULL OF ZEROES

Haunted Heart began on the radio and he turned up the volume and accelerated up the ramp and into the sunlight there that hung on Grand Ave. He nodded to the façade of the Elmwood Arms in recognition of some private thought and drove south to East 1st St. and the morning there. Then he turned south and drove the first of the ten blocks that separated him from Central Ave. He stopped when he saw Roscoe's, a diner that specialized in chicken and waffles, if there was such a combination. He parked in the lot and walked into the joint. There was a black man taking coffee at the counter, otherwise the place was empty. He sat in a green booth with an offwhite table flecked in gold. The condiments included hot sauce, which Sonny had learned over the years indicated that most of the diner's patrons were colored. Sonny couldn't have cared less. He wanted a bacon and cheese omelette with biscuits and gravy, and it made no matter who made them or who took the order. The waitress, the only one that he saw in the place, sauntered over like the world had nothing but time and stood over his table. She was beautiful in a haggard and hard way, but it was nearly indecipherable given her reckless disregard for anything approaching civility. You had to look hard. She brought with her a glass of ice water which she slid across the table to him like it was a beer in a smoky bar. Then she asked if he wanted to look at the menu since it was sitting closed in front of him. There was perhaps the hidden insinuation that Sonny wasn't looking at the menu because he couldn't read.

"No. Thanks. I'll have a bacon and cheese omelet with biscuits and gravy. And coffee."

"It look like breakfast time to you?" She asked, her head tilted to one side. It seemed a rhetorical question. Then she added, for good measure: "That's quite a right you caught."

"Yeah. It's the spring fashion. You want one?" He asked, not kidding. Sonny realized then that he could not make out her ethnic truth. She could have been Indian. African. Mexican. All of them. He gave up on the thought and looked at her with interest.

The waitress said nothing in return but seemed uncomfortable with the eye contact.

"Actually, darling," Sonny continued, "to answer your first question, it looks like the place needs *customers*, regardless of whether it's 'breakfast time'. I'll have my bacon and cheese omelet with biscuits and gravy. If the cook would like to discuss it, I'll be happy to. *You let him know*," he said. He smiled then, and it gave the waitress the chills. It was the smile of a cat in a fairy tale being asked a request.

"I mean, look, I'll tell him. We just don't do—"

"I'm *sure* you can make an exception, dear. What with y'all being so busy and all." He tapped his finger on the table and added: "And if I have so much of a *thought* that the food has been tampered with, even a thought, I'll have a private conversation with each of you. And get the coffee quick, please." He smiled again. When he looked in her eyes, he saw that she was staring at the tattoo on the underside of his right forearm depicting a black cat with its back arched and ridged fur surrounded by *Lucky 13*.

She wrote something on her pad. It did not seem like enough of an effort to accommodate the whole order but Sonny had faith. She turned then and walked away but her saunter had little of the same shake as her entrance and instead seemed given some silent motivation.

His coffee arrived quickly. It was steaming. You had to give it that. He sipped it. Then he again went over the particulars of his day. There was the conversation with Billy Banken when he arrived for work. Sonny would find out his connection with Betty and Scooter Webb and how Vinnie fit into the thing. That would be a nice conversation, or perhaps it wouldn't. It didn't really matter. Today was the day things happened. Anything on the periphery was collateral damage. Then across town to the greasy spoon and the counter girl there. To feel like a high schooler again. That was dumb, the whole thing, but even with that admission he didn't find himself taking it off the list of items on the agenda. Then to pick up Katie at 6, and to Gilmore Field and the Stars game. Then the day truly began. And he had to hit the Union Jack again. It wouldn't do but to see Mick again. He sipped his coffee. To make it through today intact might require some improvisation. And to be killed in front of Katie. Well, that would simply be unacceptable. Perhaps that *was* why he was bringing her along, he thought again, to give him the motivation to avoid dying, the fulcrum against which he could balance the fates. He smiled to himself.

The omelet arrived in pristine condition. It could have come from his own kitchen though he didn't have one at present. There had been a time, it seemed many lifetimes ago at that moment, but there had been a time when he had fancied himself a reasonable cook and barbecue man, not to mention bartender and drink mixer. Back when he had a wife and did things like dinner with friends and cocktail parties with neighbors. Where everyone sat around and talked about world affairs that would never involve them and how the high school football team was doing. Listened to ball games on the radio. Sensible things, as most folks would call them. But Back Then was a long time ago that would never be found again. As illusory as childhood.

Upon finishing this silent reminiscence he looked down and his plate was empty. The gravy had fork trails in it where he had seemingly scooped up whatever odds and ends had been left behind and would now only leave chalkboard-like scratching sounds. He lay down his fork and used the napkin to clean his lips. His coffee had been refilled, and he found some comfort in the fact that the waitress had not dumped it in his lap upon seeing his absent stare. He wondered briefly what Betty would think of him now. The attitude. A complete lack of the ambiguity of civility. But what had she ever thought of him? Hadn't he been wrong all along anyway? Did she have any idea how many quick freebies *he* could have gotten from hopped-up hookers looking to avoid lockup? But did he ever? Did any of it even matter? It was years ago, he thought, and realized he had said it out loud. He sneered at the idea of his madness.

He killed his coffee and looked up and the waitress was leaning at the end of the bar, looking at him. He smiled at her and she turned away. Somewhere, that satisfied him. He raised his check and approached the cash register.

The waitress never did look at him (though there were no other customers in the place at the time) but found her way to the register nonetheless. She looked like she had somewhere better to be, but considering her workload Sonny found that difficult to believe.

He handed her the check and said, "Everything was wonderful, thank you." He cleared his throat and continued: "If I was a bully earlier, I apologize. But if you had been nicer from the outset, things may have happened differently. The omelet was delicious. Give my compliments to the chef."

The lady of questionable ethnic lineage rang the check in and did not look up. Sonny paid her. She gave him change. He pocketed it. And still, nothing. Finally she looked past his right shoulder and said, "I aint had it easy, man. You go tell it to someone gives a damn," she nearly whispered. Her words were tired and full of a bitterness Sonny had no interest in knowing the root of.

Sonny ran his hand over his slick hair and placed a cigarette between his lips. He looked at her then, square, "Tell you what," he said. "I learned something when my wife was gunned down in our house. In our bed. Two shots in her beautiful chest. I learned right then that each moment we have here is a gift, and that's not some fuckin poem in a card. No two ways about it. If things don't work out for you, sweet thing, I'm sorry about that. But the responsibility for that is on you. *Most things don't work out*, that's just the way of it." He lit his cigarette. "The goal here aint to cheat our fate but to deal with the one we got," he said, and exhaled over her left shoulder.

She said nothing but would not meet his eyes.

He turned then and walked out, without looking back. He wondered what the time in Mexico had done to him. He had left for four years and come back to lecture the workers of Los Angeles on the philosophical underpinnings of their inadequacies. And with his pristine record, too, he reasoned. He cleared his throat and spat a wad of phlegm that went wayward immediately and onto the windshield of a Ford.

Pulling out of the parking lot, he looked at the sign, Famous for Our Chicken and Waffles, and lamented the fact that he had tried neither. This life is never long enough.

***

He drove east on 1st until Central Ave, where he turned right, heading south for the Little Harlem club. He passed the bars and barber shops and pawn shops and liquor stores and markets which looked so different in the light of day as to be unrecognizable from the previous night. Even the people looked different. Still black, or mostly so, but the flair and decadence the night demands had wilted under the scorched concrete and the sun itself. The Merc chortled and barreled forward with its casual arrogance and chrome lines and artificial California plates.

There were fewer cops during the daytime, but their presence was still a commanding one. Sonny had only been called down here once in his time with the force, and besides a few leads here and there, had little cause to make the trip. The One Time occurred shortly after the war had ended. There had been a call for All Available to Central Ave on a Sunday afternoon in late September. It had been an overreaction from the start because the force wanted to avoid another lashing like they had received from the Zoot Suit Riots. Sonny intimated the same to Harold as they drove east that day but Harold was within himself, worried about the avenue and the attention it might receive. About how that might affect the talent recruited there, and therein his leisure time.

The situation had gone down thusly: Three white Navy boys had gone into a poolroom and club and began to live it up. It all began innocently enough, with the possible exception of choice of locale, but that would check out upon reflection. They took on the house regulars and word was that one sailor could really play. Trouble was, they were also drinking like prohibition was inevitable and they were looking to store the stuff in their bladders. The eventual loss led to a claim of cheating and bum bumpers and then into a pushing match. One of the two who couldn't play pool any better than Sonny could hold a note in the shower stepped forward and claimed that they had every right to be there because his girl, who was a negro and lived around the corner, was to meet them there in half an hour. Somehow that didn't help the situation and out of some fifteen men in the melee there were two pool cues broken across the back of the same man (which the cops couldn't help but laugh at, over some review) and one cue ball thrown into a mirror. A couple of black eyes. And then the Navy men ran out of the club like their lives were in danger (which was possible, all agreed) and a passing black and white spots them, both white officers, and the situation quickly got out of hand. Sonny arrived with Harold and after being apprised of the situation they spent the bulk of the day sitting on the hood of their car, smoking cigarettes, Sonny making faces at the little kids collected at the scene. The media tried desperately to make it bigger than it was but there was nothing for it. Funny part was, the one Navy man really *did* have a black girlfriend there and she arrived after the thing had happened. Sonny had taken her statement those five years ago and remembered her as a pensive and slim girl, thoughtful in her answers. Like a young lady who very much understood the delicacy of the matter and responded with candor and grit rather than anger. Sonny was taken then with her sense of calm coupled with a pride and sense of self-worth that would not be questioned. As he drove south he wondered at the status of *that* relationship. At the intricacies and paths that each among us choose, all too aware of the odds and the irrationality of choice.

The Little Harlem club stood on the corner in silence. As if there were no people and never had been any. It looked every bit like a still life from an Edward Hopper or his ilk. It would be called *Corner on Central Ave* or something otherwise cute in the obvious and expected manner of those forced to title something best left untitled. Sonny idled at the corner, looking over at the thing like there was an answer writ on the front door. There wasn't. It seemed peaceful enough. He drove east on Imperial and then to the alley behind it and no cars there either. Sonny walked to the back door and found it locked. He didn't know why he had done that. He would have been shocked to find it otherwise.

He drove back out front and sat at the corner of Imperial and Central so that he could see the traffic in all four directions. There wasn't much in the early afternoon. He killed the engine. He killed a cigarette. After fifteen minutes, the whole thing reminded him of a stakeout, and he hated stakeouts. One of the worst aspects of the job. He listened to the radio to kill the time, but it all bored him. In the backseat, he eyed an old waterbent copy of *The Lady in the Lake.* The cover depicted a dead blonde in a purple dress and jade necklace adrift in the deep blue. She appeared to be sucking in her cheeks, which seemed to him a curious thing to be doing just then. Sonny had seen his share of floaters and none of them held a handle to her. The book had been dropped in a puddle once, warped from the sun and two pages had been ripped out when Sonny had needed them as impromptu business cards. But it was still his favorite in the Marlowe series up until '46. That was when his reading life had stopped. He didn't know what had come after that. Had there been others? He imagined there had been, and he imagined that Marlowe had clever comebacks in each of them. But *that* one. And then there was Sheriff Patton. He made the story, as far as Sonny was concerned, who loved small town Sheriff's. In another life Sonny was sure that he would become one, or had been one. Where he could be Sheriff and Fire Chief and dog catcher and best chili cook. But not in Los Angeles, and not in this life.

He looked back to the four corners. Without a partner here he couldn't read, of course. Marlowe and Sheriff Patton would have to continue to bake on the back seat. He exited the car and stood against the thing for a different view. A song came on the radio from Billie Holliday and he leaned in the driver's window and turned up the volume. He didn't know the title, but it was a good one. She had a voice Sonny could ache to. A few cigarettes later a Cadillac pulled up in front of the club. A black lady got out and kissed the driver, then walked to the front door and unlocked it. One of the three sisters who owned the thing, Sonny figured. The Brown sisters? Was that it? Sonny couldn't remember. Come in to make some calls and figure the books from the previous night. He didn't move, because none of the Brown sisters or whatever their name was meant a thing to him. There was a diner on the corner and Sonny walked there and swung open the door, keeping a close eye on Little Harlem. He got a cup of coffee to go and walked back to his car. The stuff was like whiskey—you had to have will to drink it—but once you did, it was worth it.

The day moved along and Sonny felt like he was in the elevator of the Elmwood Arms. Then a late model Ford pulled up in front of the club and parked on the street. One Billy Banken got out of the car and then moved the seat forward and rummaged through his back seat for something of importance. Sonny turned off the radio and removed the keys from the ignition and footed it across the street, quickly and quietly. With one hand he cupped the .45 in his rear waistband and found the other still clinging to the cold coffee cup. He sipped the last of the stuff and tossed the cup into the gutter. Billy had removed himself from the back seat and was walking to the front door of the club. As he arrived there, Sonny was some twenty feet behind him and moving quickly. Billy had still not turned around as he knocked on the door. Sonny stopped. The whole world stopped. Nothing happened. Then he knocked again and there was a crack along the edge of the doorway and a nod of recognition and Billy walked in then with a rough hand to his back which caused the door to jolt inward and the lady holding it to stumble backwards. Sonny grabbed the door and shut the thing and locked it behind him.

In front of him in the main room of the Little Harlem club was a woman of perhaps sixty who had fallen on her substantial behind and Billy, who was just then realizing his situation. His face had run a sprint from acknowledgement to disgust to anger to a sober realization of the odds of the thing. He stood facing Sonny, bent kneed, like a linebacker in need of some coaching.

Sonny held the .45 on both of them.

"Don't worry, darlin," he said. "I aint here to rob you. I don't want any money." Then to Billy: "You thought the big boys last night would handle me?" It was a rhetorical question, of course, and he let it hang out there and take a look.

Billy said nothing but looked for all the world like the reality he found himself in was very different from the one he had wished for.

"It aint polite to not answer questions, but I'll give you that one as a courtesy," Sonny said. "Sit down," he told the woman. "Not on the floor, either."

"You aint got to be tellin me what to do, man," the lady said as she rose from her position without help from either of them. As she walked to a chair and began sitting, she looked at Billy and asked, "This the man who roughed up Delroy and Johnny last night?" She adjusted her glasses and waited for an answer.

Billy continued staring at Sonny, bent kneed, and if the blankness portrayed on his face was an act, he was the world's first method actor.

"What the hell is wrong with you, Billy?" The lady halfshouted. Sonny looked at her and realized that though he knew little to nothing about her, he liked her nonetheless. She had a spunk to her.

Billy came to then, shook his head once and looked at her. "Yes'm," he said. "This him alright."

She turned her attention then to Sonny: "You gonna tell us what you want or you just like holding that gun on us? Make you feel like a big man? Can't just leave us alone?"

Sonny smiled at her. "When I look in the mirror naked I feel like a big man," he answered. "The gun just makes sure people mind what you say. You take it out. They listen to you. It's quite a coincidence."

She said nothing to that, but adjusted her glasses again with her right hand and tightened her lips in disapproval and looked away.

"Billy. Take a seat," Sonny said, and made it sound as if there were no other option.

He did.

"Now, is anybody else due to come in here? A janitor? T-Bone? One of your sisters? Anyone?"

The lady looked at Billy in the hopes that he would answer, and she quickly pursed her lips in disgust. Apparently he had lost the ability of speech. So she answered: "Yeah, mister. We got somebody s'posed to come in here in about a hour." She looked at her watch for confirmation. Then looked at Billy and shook her head.

"We'll be long done by then. Either way it turns out. Anyways, if you're lying, I'm shooting Billy in the kneecap." Sonny smiled and Billy looked up at him like an 8-year old looks at the bully who just acquired lunch money with only a threat. He was *hurt*. There was no other way to say it.

"Billy, you and I go way back. But you don't know it. You tipped off Big Vinnie from Mickey C's crew that my wife and Scooter Webb were dancing the horizontal foxtrot."

Both Billy and the lady's eyes lit at the name of somebody they knew well.

"It's okay, really. I'm used to the idea now." He waved the gun in the air for affect. "Now," he said, "I want confirmation from you. I want information about how you found out. I want you to search your big brain into the farthest regions and try and remember *anything* you can about the situation. Comprende?"

Billy nodded in silence.

"But in order to do this properly, you must *speak*. I have confidence in you." He pointed the gun at Billy Banken. "I also know that you were banging a white girl, a prossy named Emma at around the same time who was good friends with *my* wife. So, you see the problem I have with the situation? My wife and Scooter were killed by Big Vinnie shortly after you passed on the word. I was on the force at the time, working on Mickey C. You gettin this?"

Sonny saw that he was.

The lady was looking at Billy in a disapproving manner and shaking her head at him.

"Billy? I asked you a question. Answer in 3 seconds or I shoot you in the shoulder. Your choice. I hear it hurts. One—"

Billy ran his fingers over his face roughly and looked up. "Fine," he said. "Yeah. I get it," he said. "I get it."

The exasperation in his voice made Sonny believe him.

"Are you one of the Brown sisters, by the way?" He asked the woman.

She looked at him long and hard. There was clearly a decision being weighed there and finally she answered proudly: "Yes, sir. I *am*."

"Good. Nice joint you run here," Sonny said, and gestured at the air about him. "If it wasn't for this guy, I'd never be in your life. And that T-Bone Walker. Man's a hell of an entertainer. Got a friend who loves his act. I'm more of a Sinatra guy myself. Y'know, Tommy Dorsey, all that." He shrugged at the admission and continued: "Don't do anything stupid and you'll make tonight's show. You have my word on that." He winked at her. He paused, and nobody spoke. Then he asked: "How's the muscle from last night, by the way?"

"If you're referring to Delroy and Johnny, Delroy got a broken knee, or somesuch. He gonna be on crutches for a *long* while. Johnny got his jaw broke in two places. Thanks to you."

"Thanks to me?"

"Yes, *you*, sir."

"Yeah, that's swell," he said, and rolled his eyes at her. "Spare me the melodrama. They weren't exactly playing pattycake with me, and I didn't do a fuckin thing. I just asked *this* fucker a question. See, it all keeps coming back to him." He motioned towards Billy and continued: "I'm just glad to hear they're on the up and up," Sonny said, though he didn't look overjoyed with the admission. "Really," he added.

"I can't believe that only you did all that, be honest with you. Two men that size—." She trailed off, the words aimed at nobody in particular.

"I'm just lucky that way. And they take too much for granted because they think their size means something. You never know about a man," Sonny said and itched the underside of his chin with the barrel of the gun in his hand. "Now Billy," he said, "you aint been too forthright as of yet, and I got quite a busy schedule today. I mean, this is fun and games and all, but..."

The words trailed off into the empty club until it seemed they had never existed at all. Billy looked back at Sonny as if he would never speak. Eventually, Sonny figured, Billy would again regain the ability to formulate a sentence. And just like that, he did: "I got nothing to say to you. You aint no cop, all them tattoos and such. And if you aint no cop, you can't make me do nothin."

Sonny shot him then in the left shoulder. The blast was extraordinarily loud considering the previous moment. Billy clutched the joint immediately and rolled to the ground. Ms. Brown brought her hands up near her face though the rest of her sat still and looked from Billy to Sonny.

"Go get him a towel. Or two. Better get three," Sonny advised.

Ms. Brown stood and walked to the bar and did as she was told. When she returned, she leaned down to Billy and helped him up. Billy was whimpering and holding his shoulder. He sat down again because Sonny told him to.

"Now. What the fuck is wrong with you? I'm not a cop. Did I say I was? And how could it matter when I'm three feet from you with this thing. Gun is real." He waved it in his hand and looked at it in the hopes they would as well. "That was stupid," Sonny continued. "You're stupid. And that's not a value judgment, just a fact. Kneecap is next. Really. If you ever want to walk normal again, you *have* to talk. Now open up on the Big Vinnie thing."

Billy breathed out and a chunk of his spittle was ejected and turned over on itself like a boomerang. Both Sonny and Ms. Brown watched it sail about the room. It landed on the right arm of Sonny's shirt. They all looked at the spit there and nobody said anything. Then Billy began: "Shit, man. Didn't mean that. Yeah. I talked to Vinnie one time, but, like, years ago—"

"*Four.* Four years ago," Sonny interjected.

"Whateva, man. He come in here and aks about that girl you talked about. Emma. Says that she gonna catch a bad one 'less I got some shit for him. And Scooter, *man.*" He stopped there. He reclutched his ailing shoulder. The blood from the wound had soaked through the towel and was running in rivulets over his fingers.

"Billy, don't you even go and tell this man that you did somethin get Scooter killed. I done known you twenty years now. He was *your friend*," Ms. Brown said, as if that automatically made the concept impossible to grasp.

"He fucked you over, didn't he Billy? Took a job from you? Steal your weed?" Sonny said, and lit the cigarette that had been dangling from his seam of lips.

Billy kicked out his leg in an impotent gesture of rage like a grade schooler. He looked near tears.

"Didn't he, Billy?" Sonny persisted, and exhaled in Billy's direction.

Billy looked at Ms. Brown as if Sonny were not there and spoke to her: "Scooter had got me kicked out Gerald's band! Accused me of that drug thing so's he could take my spot! I couldn't let that happen!" He nearly shouted this at her, and stood.

"Whoa, cowboy. *Sit*," Sonny said, and gestured to the seat with the .45.

Billy looked at Sonny and licked his lips as if he thought about disobeying the order and finally sat.

Ms. Brown shook her head and looked skyward. "Lord," she said, "tell me this boy did not soil Scooter's name and drive him to his death. Tell me that, Lord." She shook her hands and held them above her head as if she expected an answer.

"So you tell Vinnie, what? How do you know this?"

Billy looked at Sonny then, as if to plead his case. As if he wanted somebody in the room to understand his plight. "I was *close* with Scooter, 'fore that," he said. "I know he be shackin up with some white chick, some cop's girl. *I didn't know the lady.* The girl I was seein, Emma, she knew her. So I tole Vinnie a little bit about it and a couple days later..."

"*Billy!*" Ms. Brown admonished, and looked anew at her old friend.

"I never meant for that to *happen*! God knows I didn't! I just thought. Well. I just thought he might scare the two of em. How could I know all this! That it was the girl of the dude checkin Mickey C out!?"

He looked from Ms. Brown to Sonny in the hopes of finding some empathy etched there somewhere. There was none present.

"That was my *wife*, Billy. I worked long hours trying to get these mobster clowns behind bars. They get the dime from you, find out it's my wife, and they plug both of them. And he tells me about it that night. You'll like this. Listen." He exhaled then between both of them and continued: "I walk in to this supper club with my partner, just to let Mickey C know we're there, you know, and Vinnie mentions that my wife ought to be walking funny. That I should really spend more nights at home. I find this out from a greaseball like him. So I go home early that night, just to check, see, and my wife and your friend are painted all over the headboard. She took two shots to the chest and him one to the head." Sonny stopped there. Looked at the two of them.

No one spoke. No one wanted to. They were all waiting for an indication as to Sonny's mood. Sonny was, too.

Then he spoke again to Billy: "That girl, Emma. She's dead now, too. Or missing. Disappeared awhile back. You didn't have anything to do with that, didya?" Sonny asked, and looked at Billy hard. He didn't expect to get an answer to this, and wondered why he had mentioned it at all.

"No sir," the man answered quickly, though Sonny saw the surprise in his eyes. "I aint seen her in 3, 4 years. I mean, you know, we had some good time, but..." He looked then at the soiled towel on his shoulder. "This shit *hurts*," he said.

"Yeah, I told you it would," Sonny said, and looked over at Ms. Brown. She had an expression like the whole room stank and she was trying not to acknowledge it. He could see the irreconcilable damage done to the relations between the two old acquaintances.

"So what do I do with you, Billy? It was your tongue that got my wife killed. Think about that a second." He left Billy a second. "That deserves some form of retribution, don't you think?" he finished.

"I didn't know that he would—"

"You tell a known mobster and Mickey Cohen associate about a cop's wife banging a jazzman, and a negro at that, and expect nothing to happen? I admit that I think you're stupid, Billy. But you aint *that* dumb. Near nobody is. And I *know* you don't think *I'm* stupid enough to believe that."

"Look, man—." He was pleading. Sonny looked at Ms. Brown, who had washed her hands of the thing completely. She was no longer scared but simply disgusted with the both of them. She wore it on her face like cheap foundation.

Sonny stood quickly and pistolwhipped Billy across the jaw to the left and then the right. He felt multiple teeth leave their bearings and Billy looked up at Sonny with tearful eyes and a bloody mouth. He started to form a word that rattled and stopped at the base of its inception. Then he looked down. His mouth leaked onto the floor and formed a small pool of crimson around a tiny archipelago of teeth.

Sonny said nothing because he was playing this whole thing badly and he knew it. He looked over at Ms. Brown and she stood still in her chair, gazing intently at Billy. "*You deserve worse*," Sonny said then to Billy, though the words felt awkward and inadequate. He was sure there were better words for the moment but he didn't know any. He wasn't going to kill this man. Whatever morality had been muddied in Mexico would not stain this afternoon. Billy wanted no ill will for Betty, didn't even know her. Sonny looked towards the bar to gather himself and then once to Ms. Brown, who met his gaze. There was something in it that unsettled Sonny. He walked to the door then, without looking back. Behind him, he heard the woman stand and walk over to Billy who began to sob without shame like a child. Sonny unlocked the door from the inside and walked into the brilliant spring sunshine of Los Angeles, as unsure of his actions in the immediate past as those in the distance hardly recalled but from which he still felt the sting and acrid smell of their recoil.

A TRUNK FULL OF ZEROES

14.

He started the engine to the Merc and turned the radio up. He bowed his

head at his inept handling of the Little Harlem club and wondered at the

price he would pay if he continued to run the streets of Los Angeles

throughout the day like he was the only man in the city with a gun. He

made a circuitous u-turn in the street and headed west on Imperial

Highway. Nat King Cole sang *Sweet Lorraine* through the speakers; the

smell of barbecue swept in through the open window; palm trees lined the

sidewalks and the sky was cloudless; it was all a perfect Southern California

day to cap the greaseball who killed your wife, Sonny figured. He sneered

at the false promise of the city and pushed his foot down on the accelerator

and the beast under the hood wailed like a primordial being loosed upon the

modern world

There was no getting around it, he figured. His handling of things

to the present point had been sloppy, unprofessional, even lazy. Tonight

would have to be different. He said it out loud, and though he hadn't meant to, it sounded like there was something to it. Which he liked. Now he was going to see a girl. He had to repeat that to himself because it sounded too absurd to entertain otherwise. What am I *thinking*, he asked himself, though he never actually considered a route that would take him off his present course to West Los Angeles. I am a foolish man, he thought, and lit another cigarette to confirm it. The voice on the radio said that the previous tune had been by Artie Shaw. Artie Shaw, thought Sonny, what the hell. The guy looks like a Maytag salesman and bags both Lana Turner *and* Ava Gardner. Musicians. Go figure. He smiled nonetheless at the thought of it. Flicked his ash out the open window. He looked at himself in the rearview mirror and The Eye, purple and yellow and swollen in its socket. Then he thought of Miryea again and it all went to hell.

It had been some time since Sonny had been with a woman. For any length of time, at least. There had been a woman in Mexico for a short time. Her name had been Xiomara, and in retrospect Sonny believed that he had liked her name more than he ever did her. Nevertheless, theirs had been a shortlived though not unentertaining affair. Full of acrobatics, it had lasted maybe three months. It ended in a bar on an evening full of moon when she tossed her margarita into his face. He had no idea why she had done that, and never did learn. He spoke little Spanish and she little English and they had talked little as it was. And then, of course, his wife previously. The women he had known in a prurient fashion before her were so long ago they served only as signposts in his memory. And, he reasoned, his wife had actually been fucking someone else while they were married, so that part of the relationship *must* not have been quite doing it for her. None of these were good reasons, or perhaps reasons in any sense, as to why he should show up at the workplace of a mute Mexican girl with a murder to commit and a second purple head growing from his eye socket. Yet the Mercury cruised Northwest as if it needed no navigation at all.

North to Pico Blvd, then west, and the sign there in the distance. He wiped his forehead with his sleeve. *This is pathetic. She's gorgeous. This is a colossal mistake. I'm an idiot. My wife.* Each of these thoughts collected one atop another until they constituted nothing more than the uncollected rubble of gibberish. He parked in the lot. He looked at himself in the rearview mirror; he was still there, just as much a lug as ten minutes ago. He tested his inflated eye as if his finger was a cold compress. The swelling hurt to touch. He looked in the diner and saw it mostly empty but he saw through the window that the brown woman at the counter was looking out at him. And here he was, posing like a pretty boy in his rearview mirror and she staring at him. He left his hat on the seat and tossed his .45 into the glove compartment and quickly opened the door and walked the lot down, and he walked it as if he were being watched. It was a runway walk for the tough guy, all casual affectation and nonchalance.

The door swung open as a couple left and he held the door open and he was so loopy that he nearly smiled at them.

His heart was beating quickly but he couldn't stop to think about it. He had learned that throughout his history of extracurricular activities. Keep moving and don't overthink. Let your training take over. Except he had no training for this. She was sitting on the stool and she smiled at him and the day was no longer a loss. He smiled back and tried to stop himself because he hated his smile but couldn't stop so he looked out the window, grinning like blue skies were the cause of his happiness, or perhaps simplemindedness. That muse be it, he thought. Then he remembered she couldn't talk and when he looked back at her she was trying to write something on a napkin. He cupped her chin and gently elevated it with his hand until she was looking at him.

"Can you take a break? Can we talk a minute?" he asked. She looked towards the double doors as if an answer were writ there. Sonny knew she was looking for the cook.

"You know what, *I'll* ask him," he said.

She said nothing, of course, but reached her hand up gently towards his face and ran it about the outline of his purple eye. She looked at him with a question and he answered, "Yeah, this guy last night. I was hoping you wouldn't notice." She smiled at that because she would have to be blind as well as mute to miss it. And even then maybe not. "I'm

gonna—," Sonny said, and pointed towards the kitchen.

He walked over to the end of the counter and made his way behind

it and split the double doors and there the innards of the diner. The cook

was standing at the grill, flipping a hamburger. He looked at Sonny as if a

customer walking into his kitchen were par for the course.

"Was I not fast enough for you out there? And what, you a

regular now?" The cook said, and shrugged.

"I'm not really hungry. Look, I was hoping I could ask the

Mexican girl some questions out there. I'm working on this case—"

"You a dick?" The cook asked. He looked Sonny over as if he had

not seen him before, then back at his grill.

"Yeah. Sorta. Private, though. Anyway, could I take her outside

for a minute? I need to, I think she might be in danger—"

"No shit, man? She's Cuban, by the way. Aint Mexican. Yeah. I

guess. Go ahead and ask away, just take a pad with you. She don't really

talk."

"Is that right?"

"Yeah. Whaddya they call that, mute? Anyway. Could I see a

badge, by the way? And how do you know she's involved?" The cook

asked.

Sonny looked at the man a moment. "Well," he said, "there is a record of a Miryea being at the location of an incident that matches her description. That's really all I can say about it. Client privilege, and all." Then he reached into the back pocket of his trousers and pulled his long terminated LAPD badge. Since his departure was unusual, to say the least, he had not turned it in. He flashed it and put it away. From where the cook stood, it looked much more authentic than anything he would have thought a private dick would carry.

"So I'm just gonna—"

"Yeah, bud. Just try not to be too long. We aint busy right now, but we're gonna get a rush here in awhile." He smiled. "I been tellin myself that since I opened the joint."

Sonny grinned back and bit his tongue. He didn't mind the cook. The world was mostly assholes and elbows, and here was a guy who wasn't gonna hurt it much, Sonny figured. He turned and walked out to the front area. There were two couples sitting in booths. Otherwise the place was empty.

When he reached the front counter, he leaned his two hands against it and looked at her. "Let's go outside and talk a minute," Sonny said. "I already arranged it with your boss."

She smiled at him and looked once at the double doors to the kitchen and then stepped out from behind the counter carefully, like she was cheating on a test for the first time and awkwardly trying to avoid notice.

She wore a blue dress with white polka dots that had seen better days as the fringes and seams frayed with age. She wore it, however, like it was made for her, all rounded curve and grace. Her hair was tied simply in the back but the front had been flipped and molded and shaped in ways that would forever remain a mystery to Sonny. Where men have created empires and invented mythology and fought silly wars, the manipulation of a top full wave reverse roll through pincurls and backcombing remained the stuff of legend. There was a white scarf tied around her neck that offset her tanned skin in ways men enjoyed thinking about. They still do. Miryea stopped before she reached the front door and turned and pointed towards the rear of the place and the door there.

"You wanna go in back?" Sonny asked. Miryea nodded, and began walking there. Sonny stood and watched her leave, forgetting for the moment that he was supposed to follow.

The alley in the back of the joint smelled of spoiled produce. Sonny smiled to himself. No matter where he went he seemed to spend most of his time in the dark and rancid alley behind it. Miryea looked at Sonny and smiled and put her hand to her nose and plugged her nostrils and scrunched her brows in mock disgust all at once. Sonny took out a cigarette because he was terrified to think about what he should say to a beautiful mute girl and so involved himself in repetition. There is no manual for this, he thought, and if there is, I haven't read the damn thing. She reached her hand out and he placed a cigarette in it and lit it for her. He felt rude and oaffish for not offering her one. This was not an uncommon sensation for Sonny when around beautiful women, feeling awkward and oaffish. The exception was Katie but that was simply because she was family and because he was unable to accept the fact that she had grown and still viewed her as a little girl. They walked to the mouth of the alley with the Southern California sunshine about them and the saturated warmth of the concrete upon their soles. It was not uncomfortable somehow, which Sonny found astonishing. It was all astonishing, really. Who is this girl? And where the hell am I walking with her? He found himself thinking.

"Sorry about my eye," he said, for lack of a better thing to say. "I mean, not that I'm pretty anyway, but—yeah. I'm an idiot." He ran his hand over his hair as a gesture of deflecting his embarrassment. He knew that he was beet-red and wondered how he was going to get through this. He didn't like talking. She couldn't talk.

At the end of the alley, they made a left onto the sidewalk, both unawares as to an actual destination. They killed their cigarettes and tossed them into the gutter. The street was lined on either side with single story stucco Spanish revival homes that populated Southern California like they were Catholic themselves. None of them looked particularly impressive but they all shared a certain quality of cute and comfortable. The palm trees with moppish hairdos and scarred trunks loomed like the world's largest flowers. Miryea looked up at them and backed onto the sloped lawn of one of the houses and sat there. Sonny looked at her, unsure as to whether the move was permanent.

She clapped her hands softly at him to get his attention and motioned with her finger for him to sit next to her. He walked to the driveway and saw no car there and no motion in the windows and assumed nobody home and so sat. She laughed at him for his caution. Sitting on the ground was not a comfortable action for Sonny, as with many middleaged men, and so he searched until he found a position that did not hurt some part of him. Miryea looked at him throughout this laborsome process like he was a creature unlike she had ever had fortune to witness. The ankle holster popped in and out of sight as he moved his leg. She noticed it, looked at it and then him. He grinned at her like he had been caught and covered it back up with his pant leg.

"You're young still," he said, by way of explaining his difficulty with the contortions.

She smiled and held up two fingers on one hand and three on the other.

"You're 23? Yikes," Sonny said.

She shook her head and laughed silently at his folly.

"Not *32*," he said incredulously. His forehead shrunk into three horizontal creases that demonstrated his disbelief.

She nodded, and pointed at Sonny for his age.

"No way you're 32. You're not a day over 25," he said. "No way." Sonny had no natural talent with flattery but his honesty made her blush, her sunbrowned cheeks wearing rouge previously unseen. "Huh," he remarked.

She looked down at her feet and pulled some blades of grass from there.

"I'm 42," he said, finally. "And some days I feel every minute of it. Like when I have to sit on a lawn." He smiled. "Anyway," he looked skyward as he talked, "the cook told me you were from Cuba. How long you been here?"

She looked at him and extended two fingers. Then she reached that hand towards his face and placed it flat against his left cheek and ear while her thumb softly outlined the swelling on his eye. She kept her hand pressed there until he feigned pain and removed it. They made eye contact and smiled each to each.

Then she grabbed her pad that had been placed next to her on the grass and ripped out a page and handed it to Sonny. On it were written the words: *You remind me of the men I grew up seeing in Cuba.*

"I'm that old, huh?" Sonny looked at her with a scrunched brow. "Doesn't say much for the fellas in Cuba then," he said and grinned. His grin was much more natural than his smile, which looked in actuality like a grimace. The grin contained a hint that perhaps he knew more than you ever would, regardless of the situation. The grin had given him an upper hand in many difficult situations over the years. His smile looked as if it contained the weeping of the world within it.

She swatted him on the arm softly at his remark and pretended to be hurt.

"So what about me reminds you of them? I mean, when you saw me yesterday? I'm just some lug that walks into a coffee shop."

She scribbled on the pad and then stopped. She chewed on the end of the pencil in thought and included something else. Then she ripped it off and gave it to Sonny with a smile. The sheet read: *you seem confident. Like you know something we don't.*

"Ha," Sonny blurted out. "I'm confident that I'll mess up any situation I step in. I'm confident that I have no business being in the same room with a woman with half the looks you do." He smiled at her then, but it was an honest smile forced by the instant and not one so constructed after a compliment. "No, darlin," he went on, "there are very few things in this world I do well." He ripped from its moorings a small tuft of grass and tossed it over his shoulder. "And most of those involve hurting people in some way or another. That's just the way it is."

He looked at her and she was focused intently on his face. She wore neither a smile nor a frown. If Sonny had meant to scare her, he found then that she was perhaps sturdier than he had given her credit for. "I sound like a sap," he continued. "I've had it good and I've had it bad. What're you gonna do?" he asked, rhetorically.

She wrote on her pad then. She handed him the sheet. *My husband was military in Cuba and gone now five years ago. It took a long time to accept. Everyone gets the bad.*

He looked up at her then and felt embarrassed for droning on about his misfortune. He nodded to her and said, "I lost my wife too. Four years ago. I'm still figuring it all out."

They looked away from each other then, both of them focused on some small center in a distance otherwise unseen. An easterly wind reordered the day and Miryea stood. She looked down at Sonny in a way that made him look away again. She picked up her pad and wrote on it and handed it to Sonny. Before he could read it, she ran her hand over his cheek and turned and walked away. It was all one motion and as fluid as water. He nearly called after her but didn't and instead glanced down onto the paper on which was writ her name and an address.

A TRUNK FULL OF ZEROES

***

He sat on the grass and looked up at the sky and squinted his eyes at the bright afternoon. Light would be failing soon. What he wanted was a *drink*. He could see it then as he had so often in the black past, the gold rimmed glass tipped with the ceaseless flicker of neon reflecting atop the fullness of it. Girls who would drink down the moon and dance upon the tables to do it sat stooled on either side of him. The nirvana and numbsoul desire. The sweat of a cold beer chaser. He looked northward for strength though he felt like a gambler that had never seen a winning streak. He began to breathe deeply, focusing on relaxing. As if it were a thing tangible to be plucked from the air. He looked down again. She had left an address. Sonny didn't pretend to have learned much in this world but one thing he knew for certain was that he would be visiting that address if he couldn't get that drink. As he contemplated a way to fit in an extra stop on an evening already so full with engagements, a Ford pulled into the same driveway on whose lawn he sat. *Of course*, Sonny thought, though he made the conscious attempt to display no reaction at all.

The driver was a man wearing a wide-brimmed brown hat and a shirt open at the collar. Thick black hair curled out from the opening. It was a strange thing to notice. The driver stared straight ahead as he entered the drive, then stopped the car and looked out the window at

201

Sonny. There was an instant of recognition in which Sonny discerned that the man pulling into the driveway was not an honest citizen returning home early to surprise his wife and treat her to dinner. He wasn't surprised enough to see Sonny sitting there, and he had the telling and vacuous look of so many thugs Sonny had dealt with over the years. There was little but basic intelligence there, without the clutter of pesky morality to disturb it.

In the moment Sonny folded back his pant leg and reached for the holster there, the man had opened the door and was exiting in one smooth motion onto a knee. Each man pulled off a round before either had proper balance or aim. The rear tire some three feet from the man popped a hole and began hissing loudly and was drumflat in an instant. Sonny went into a single roll then down the sloped lawn and in that time the thug fired twice more, one bullet ricocheting sharply off the sidewalk. As Sonny came to rest upon a single knee, he fired three times. The first shot missed wide right again but the second and third were true. The man bucked with each slug and fell into a reclining position in the door, mouth agape. Sonny kept his gun out and footed it quickly towards the car. Only one shot left in this thing, he thought, and raised it as if it would bear reflection. The man looked asleep—as in the absence of a chaise lounge he regularly used the frame of his car door to recline. The slugs had struck within two inches of one another in the area of the man's heart. They bled each to each, his shirt slicked in crimson.

Sonny donned the man's hat and grabbed him by the collar and dragged him to the lawn. He lay facedown there, anonymous in death as in life. Sonny wondered briefly at the owner of the house who would come home to find a corpse on his lawn. Sonny had not recognized the man, but that meant nothing. Four years was an eternity. Neighbors had come out of their houses and were standing on sidewalks attempting to be discreet while staring. Sonny did not acknowledge them. The situation was so out of control at this point that the only thing to bring the day down further would be for a witness to get a good luck at his face. He slanted the brim of the dead man's hat over his eyes and sat in the driver's seat of the car. The keys hung from the ignition and he calmly turned the engine over and backed out the drive, the left rear tire flapping like a thing alien entire.

At the corner he made a right onto Pico Blvd and drove the block west slowly in a stunted slapping rhythm. He saw his car in the parking lot of the diner and directed the Ford that way. He parked it in front of a fire hydrant, wiped the steering wheel and handles down with a handkerchief and left the car there, idling. He again pulled the hat down over his eyes and made for the Mercury. The sirens had begun though he placed them two to three minutes from arrival and he opened his car door and keyed the ignition. He did not look into the diner and hoped Miryea had not spotted him deliberately trying to avoid detection, but things were as they were at that point. The moon now hung pendant but without darkness to accompany it and the day rode on. He backed out of the parking lot and drove Pico Blvd west though that was not the direction he needed.

He doubled back some two blocks later in case he had been watched as he left and drove Olympic Blvd east into the heart of the city. He tossed the dead man's hat out of the window like a Frisbee and donned his own eight-panel snapcap. As he drove, he reasoned as to who had tried to kill him. He didn't know the man, didn't recognize him. Was he an operative for Cohen? Or personally connected with Vinnie? Sonny assumed one of those must be true. But right out in the open, in a quiet neighborhood? It didn't make any sense. If the hit was that open, then he was anybody's lay. That was comforting. Tonight had to finish it. He would take Katie and the suitcase and the Merc down to New Orleans and do what he should do for the kid. It all sounded great in theory. But first he had to see the Union Jack again. To see Mick, and, in truth, to be near the drowning gold of the spirits he had come to represent for Sonny.

***

The Merc turned left onto La Brea and there north to Sunset Blvd. Daylight was slipping away and had taken on a burnt orange glow particular to spring in Los Angeles. Neon signs had begun to battle the dusk, turquoise and red and white, a bastard constellation aligned across the belly of concrete. Sonny lit a smoke and looked at Shiv's .22 that lay on the passenger seat. Such a little thing, really. He was lucky that he was close and had hit the thug near the heart. Otherwise, the .22 may not have done it and he would have had to run like a little girl away from the neighborhood bully. He smiled at the thought. He wouldn't have made twenty feet, he knew.

Right onto Sunset then and the sky blackening down. A thin horizon of orange spread across the underside of the darkness like every day was Halloween. The Union Jack was on the left and Sonny flipped a u-turn and parked at an expired meter in front. He left the .22 in the glove box and fitted the .45 into the back of his waistband. He wouldn't be leaving that behind again.

The inside of the place was blacker than the night would ever be, the hazy red globes reminiscent of a cave. Sonny stood in the doorway as he parted the crimson drapery and let his eyes adjust.

"Christ almighty, willya look at what the almighty shat out and dropped in my pub!" Mick bellowed.

Sonny smiled at his old friend's voice and made his way to the bar. So far as he discerned there were two other men in the room, neither of which seemed a concern. The legitimacy of the wayward and addicted. He sat on the red plastic cushion of a stool and slapped the bar once.

"Manhattan, rocks," he said.

Mick grabbed him by the back of the neck and pulled his head forward like he was going to kiss him but stopped short. He examined Sonny with his one eye. "Ya need to learn how to fight," he said. "Ya damn near got yer eyeball punched through yer 'ed!" He set off laughing then, and continued for what seemed longer than what was expected. The delicate balance between decency and friendship.

"Yeah, tell me about it," Sonny said. "You try and sleep with this thing. Got any coffee?"

"No I ain't got any bloody coffee. And why would I have coffee at 5 o'clock? But I can make ya some." He whistled then to the back of the place, the kind of whistle every man who cannot wishes he could. "Ray! Look who just picked hisself off the canvas!" Then he turned and took to making a pot of coffee.

Moments later the mulatto man halved the beaded curtain that led to the rear rooms and entered. He wore suspenders atop a white shirt with black trousers below. The brown hat sat atop his head aslant and forward pitched. There was a toothpick in his mouth and a gun in his belt. He smiled at Sonny as he approached.

"You again?" He asked.

"LA can't get rid of me. It's tryin though," Sonny said, and reached for the cup he didn't yet have. Pulled his hand back.

"Bollocks. Los Angeles *needs* blokes like us. Otherwise, it's a bunch of stuffed shirts and shitty dreams, man." He nodded towards Sonny's head. "I had one like that one time. Aches like the devil, yeah?"

He smiled as befitted the man with two heads.

"Ya seen yer girl, lad?" Ray asked, and sat on the stool next to Sonny. He took his hat off and ran his hand front to rear over his slicked back curls.

"This mornin. Yeah." Sonny paused, thinking about the question. Then he asked it anyways: "What was it you two meant with her all fancied up?"

Ray looked at Mick and him back and they each to each. The old Englishman looked like something indecent had been said. Mick walked the bar down and placed a pint of beer on the countertop in front of Ray. The ale rolled gently over the rim and onto the wood, white suds like snail tracks along the side of it. Sonny stared at it, longingly. Ray noticed and smiled. "I heard you was on the wagon, Sonny. That so?" He winked, and added: "Looks like you're doing just fine." He smiled.

"Yeah. Ain't had a drink in near four years, give or take." Sonny said, looked away.

"I'll take em," Ray answered, and brought the ale to his lips.

"I heard I wasn't too good on it," Sonny said and grinned.

"No shit? And who told you that, the whole *fucking city?*" The last word elongated, like a dragon in a Chinese New Year's Parade. Then: "You were the worst bloody drunk I ever saw, no offense man, and you were never sober." His cockney accent took away the *er* and replaced it with a soft *a* and made the word sound new again. "I remember one time you saw some scag slap a skirt up and you cleaned him a good one and dragged him near to the stage and then booted him onto the thing." He smiled at the recollection. "Poor lad didn't have the sense to stay put and when he tried to stand you threw 'im into the drum kit and grabbed one a them cymbals and pounded his head with it like you was trying out for the band. All the while the lady who got hit was poundin' you on the bloody head to let the bloke go," Ray said, and shook his head at the memory of it. "Man, that was gory. An' I got to clean the thing meself, Son. Not to mention the drummer who was havin' a fag in back wasn't too pleased. Remember that, do ya?"

Sonny shook his head. He didn't remember much. The couple years before his Betty had been killed were a blur unless he was with her. He had heard the stories. From Mick. Ray. Katie. Emma. Harold. They all had stories on Sonny's dime and it was he who was broke.

"I'm sure he remembers all them days, don'tcha Sonny?" Mick said, not so much as a question. He placed a mug of steaming hot coffee on the counter. "And that's why he's sober now. And between us, lad, what would do ya some good is a spot o' tea—not this coffee nonsense."

Sonny looked at the mug to make sure it was coffee and sipped it still steaming.

"So again, boys, what'd you need Katie for this morning,?" Sonny asked. He sipped double and pulled a cigarette from behind his ear and lit it.

"I had a meetin' with an investor this morning. He's played some hands in here before and took a likin to the girl. It's all angle and bullshit, Son. I just thought—"

"Don't do it again," Sonny interrupted. His words contained a finality unwelcome in friendly speech.

Mick raised his eyebrows at being stalled in his own joint. "He's gonna give us the cash, Sonny," he said as a way of reasoning. "We're buyin' the place next door, it's twice the footage. We're gonna have three rooms in the back and—"

"Good. Honestly, I mean it. That's great. And I can't wait to see it. But don't do it again. She's not a whore, she's not a mannequin, and she's not her mother," he said, then smoked and exhaled and sipped.

Mick looked at Ray and neither spoke.

It was clear to Sonny that Mick had not taken to Sonny's tone but this was a non-negotiable. If Sonny was to take care of the girl, it was to be on his terms.

Mick lowered his head and cupped Sonny on the shoulder once and walked away, neither humbled nor angry.

Ray leaned over to Sonny. "He was just tryin' to get the wheels in motion, man. He didn't mean nuttin by it," he said, and sipped his beer.

Sonny nodded once. Sipped. Smoked. Then he asked, "What're you drinkin?"

Ray looked at his half empty pint glass. "Fullers. London. Bloody. Pride," he answered, as if each word comprised a world entire.

***

Upon 5:30, Sonny gutted the dregs of his coffee and stood. Mick looked at him and Sonny waved him over.

"No hard feelings about earlier?"

"None, Son."

"I just don't want her," he paused and searched for words then, and gesticulated with his arms and said, "I don't want her following in her mom's footsteps. I won't let her."

Mick nodded and said nothing.

"Hey. I, shit, *we*, might be headin out tonight for a bit. May have to."

Mick nodded.

"I'll come by late tonight if I can. Gotta drop Katie off for a bit. That okay?"

"Got some business to attend to then?" He winked at Sonny once, quickly, and turned serious at once. "I'll make sure I'm here late," he said, and shook his head. "Yer such a fucker," he said. "We were all just getting along just fine without ya, ya know?" He asked the question but they both knew it rhetorical and he finished the exchange with an exhale heavier than breath.

Sonny put his hand out to shake and Mick shook it and took the bills folded there within.

"Good luck, Son," Mick said, and winked his only eye.

"Shit," Sonny answered. "I'mma need it."

They smiled each to each and parted. Outside lay the graceless symmetry of the Los Angeles sidewalk in the early night.

***

Katie was expecting him at 6 pm. It was 5:50 as he neared the outskirts of Downtown and the lower rim of the sky was of the last embers of a

211

furnace. The rest had blackened down. Sonny wasn't pleased with the fact that he had told Katie to wait outside with her bags as it was getting dark. Just another moment of brilliance in a day full of them, Sonny reasoned. He turned the corner and the Elmwood Arms there, no sign of his girl. He pulled in front where a valet should be for any hotel worth checking into and let the car idle. Katie walked out of the front doors with Chuck. He was carrying her bag over his shoulder and smiling at her like he was getting paid for doing it.

"You become simpleminded since this morning?" Sonny asked the young man.

Chuck looked at Sonny and then dropped his gaze like a stone upon understanding the question. Katie slapped Sonny on the shoulder for being rude.

"No sir, just thought you might like it if I escorted her to the car," Chuck said.

"Yeah," Sonny replied. "That *was* nice. Really. I'm an asshole. Throw the bag in the back."

Katie got into the passenger seat and Chuck fitted the suitcase onto the backseat and backed away onto the sidewalk. She leaned over Sonny and looked out at Chuck and blew him a kiss. "Thanks a bunch, and good luck," she said.

Chuck waved and was not finished waving as Sonny put the Merc into drive and pulled away from the curb. They drove west, Chuck still waving.

"That kid's got the hots for you," Sonny said to Katie, and tried to gauge a reaction on her face.

"You think?" Katie said, Sonny thought facetiously. Then: "He's a nice guy."

"There are no nice guys," Sonny said, and lit a cigarette.

" *You're* nice," the girl answered, and looked out her passenger window. Sonny said nothing to that, had no words for the amount of wrongness it contained. He exhaled and looked over at her to meet eyes, to connect in a human way and reconstruct the machinery of the moment, but she continued looking out the window and the passing dusk of Los Angeles.

A TRUNK FULL OF ZEROES

15.

They drove west on Beverly Blvd. In the distance shone the glare of

Gilmore Field, the ballpark of the Hollywood Stars. Seeing the lights,

Sonny recalled immediately how he and Betty would take in a few games a

season just a handful of years ago, how they would sit in their regular seats

over the third base dugout, how she would lean her head against his

shoulder and they would eat cotton candy off the stick. Back when times

were simpler and dinosaurs ruled the earth. How he and Betty had taken

Katie on some summer nights to Gilmore Field to wile away a neverending

youth long finished. How he was now preparing to use the ballgame to

locate and follow the man who was partially responsible for his wife's death

and shadowed his everyday. To erase what *was* with what *should be*.

How he wanted little at all to do with a baseball game tonight and more

indeed with looking down at Vinnie while the fat man choked out his last

bloodbubble of breath and extinguished the night. While some may have

lamented the deterioration of such roses for the present, to Sonny it seemed a natural progression, given the momentum of his life since 1946. His days had become a freefall without bottom and tonight would provide the apotheosis for whatever depths his imagination sought. The lights were a blur against the window.

"You still with me, cowboy?" Katie asked, and she snapped her fingers as if to pull him from some ventriloquist's spell, smiling and not unhappy to have caught Sonny so distant from the moment.

He looked at her, then again, and said nothing. He knew that he had been thinking of things that had no business reappearing tonight. She would need protection, from both Vinnie and possibly himself, and he needed the clarity to recognize that. Nothing he had done so far in Los Angeles indicated to him that he was capable of it anymore. Why hadn't he just dropped her off at Mick's? He shook his head and nearly smirked at the folly of romanticizing what no longer existed. He had to drop her off for a spell at the end of the night anyhow. "*Moron*," he said aloud.

"You okay over there, Sonny?" Katie asked, this time without the smear of sarcasm that partnered much of her speech.

Sonny smiled and lied. "Yeah, sweetie. I'm good," he said. "I was just thinkin about some old times. Remember when Betty and I would bring you here some nights? When you was about, what, 8, 10?" He looked at her and saw enough recognition to continue.

"I was just thinkin about how times have changed a bit. That's all," he said.

She nodded and looked down; pulled her knee up close to her on the seat. Then she looked out the window as the Merc idled in the muddied traffic that eventually bled into the parking lot.

Sonny continued: "Tonight, uh, could get a little dangerous if I'm not careful. And sometimes I'm not careful." He looked at her then with an expression that could only be embarrassment. "It's very important to me that you listen to my instructions, you understand? Look at me, kid." He waited for her to look at him. He asked again: "*You understand?* Tonight is gonna be what it is, but it's gonna be a fuckuva lot worse if you don't listen to me."

"I got it, Sonny," she said simply, and wiped the back of her hand across her cheek. It may have been a tear. It may have been an itch. Sonny couldn't tell, and he didn't ask. He flicked the longdead cigarette nub into the dark.

"When the night is done," he said, choosing his words singly, "we're gonna be on our way to New Orleans. I'll tell you more about it once we're on the road. I want you to keep that in mind tonight. We might not see Los Angeles for awhile. So keep your eyes open for it."

"Keep my eyes open for *what?*" She turned to him then, her sharp tongue more indicative of her age than she would have liked.

"For LA, little angel. You won't see it for awhile." Sonny smiled then, absurdly, against the pull they both felt.

"I've seen it all before, Sonny. Don't worry," she said, and resigned herself again to the window.

Sonny thought that the admission probably held more truth in it than he would have cared to admit, and was saddened by it. They inched forward as the herd advanced ever so slowly to its resting place in the parking lot.

***

They had parked their car and purchased their tickets at the window and a program from the vendor and were making their way to the seats Sonny had requested. He knew that he had to see into and above the Stars dugout, over the third baseline to the seats Cohen had owned for years, yet not be close enough for unwanted attention. He knew the addition of his body art and Katie as escort would make that unlikely under any but the most extreme circumstances, but he wanted no risk regardless.

The lights cast onto the field of American youth and the smell of cut grass brought back nostalgia Sonny didn't know existed. He had been a ballplayer in his youth in Tennessee, and recalled briefly the summer days spent sweating the Southern heat through his skin in the outfield. He and his pal Jimmy Morringer would wad sunflower seeds in their cheek like squirrels and find the pickup game at one of the nearby fields, Griffith Yard or Jackson Park. They had both been taught, as had most boys in the South, that Ty Cobb was the best baseball player that had ever donned the woolen flannel and billed cap—and his greatness was seen through the 12 batting titles and being a child of the South itself (The Narrows, Georgia, to be specific, a town neither boy had ever been to but whose qualities to produce Baseball Gods had taken on mythic meaning nonetheless). Thus, they would spit their seeds and tilt their caps slightly to the left and squint like they had seen in pictures, all neurotic superstitions and hand-me-down lore through which the boys were sure would refine their skills. There would be a break of sorts in 1923, the year Lou Gehrig debuted for the Yankees, as Sonny would then adopt both the player and man as an idol. This was blasphemy to Jimmy and many of the other boys in Blount County, Tennessee, but Sonny had been an Iron Horse man ever since. Upon his death in 1941, Sonny remembered droning on to Harold without end in the car about the man's accomplishments, and how the world would never quite recover from the loss. He finished the lecture with the point that nobody had ever missed Ty Cobb upon his passing, and he had an argument there. But Gehrig, he reasoned, had been a man worth rooting for.

A TRUNK FULL OF ZEROES

The Stars program featured a smiling Frankie Kelleher with a bat in his hand and the 'PCL Champions 1949' pennant in the background. The Oakland Oaks, the Stars opponent this opening day, was on the field warming up. Katie leaned her head over and lay it on Sonny's shoulder and the night began with but the smallest of gestures.

As the 1st inning moved quietly into the 2nd, Sonny had two concerns: 1. That Mickey Cohen or any of his cohorts had not shown above or in the dugout, and 2. the Hollywood Stars, his adopted team, were wearing SHORTS with kneehigh socks for a baseball game. The fact that he thought they all looked like they belonged in a swimming pool (really, the only reasonable excuse for an adult man to wear shorts, in his estimation) was something unto itself, and the crowd's reaction to the new uniforms seemed apathetic at best. There was a buzz upon taking the field, then nothing. He had mentioned it with disdain to Katie and she shrugged her shoulders and continued taking in the sights. *Christ*, he thought, shorts at a baseball game. Might as well get those girls out there who played during the war.

It was when the Oaks center fielder doubled home the first run of the night in the 3rd that Sonny first spotted Mickey, walking to his seats while saluting the adoring masses about him. Vinnie was with him, as was another spaghetti-head he didn't recognize. Probably a new guy. Sonny had imagined there had been a lot of new guys in four years.

Mickey was looking good. He wore a black pinstripe suit with a red flowered tie and a gray fedora. He had put on a few pounds, but Mickey was a short and robust man to begin with, so the added weight merely solidified what he already was. Vinnie, on the other hand, was still decidedly not thin. He had been fat in 1946, and in that regard time had not advanced. He looked every bit of his 6' 4" frame as he approached the seats. The third greaseball looked like a factory sort. Short, thick, hairy, stupid. He wore an illfitting suit and his smile seemed more scowl than anything. A new recruit sent from Chicago, Sonny figured.

***

Katie saw Sonny giving undue attention to the Italian men sitting some three sections from them and knew then that the beginnings of the night were taking shape. She recognized one of the men from newspapers, but could not recall the name. She didn't much pay attention to that stuff, seeing the newspaper as primarily redundant adult failures surrounding the funny pages. But she *had* seen the nattily dressed one before. Everyone seemed to like him—they stood as he passed and shook hands when they could, patted his shoulder if he had already moved past them. Los Angeles

has always been a city for the few, and Mickey Cohen fit that category.

Sonny stared at them briefly, then patted Katie on the elbow.

"Keep an eye on them all night. But don't look at 'em. If one of

'em leaves, take note of it. Tell me, if I'm gone." He half whispered these

dictums, as if their recognition alone brought unwanted attention.

Katie nodded once, then looked back at the game. At the men in

shorts. She looked over to the Mobsters, which is what she assumed they

were—they certainly *looked* like they were, and then to the field. Some of

the men *did* look quite good in those shorts, she thought, particularly that

third baseman. So, while Mickey and his entourage provided the necessary

eyesore for Sonny, Katie focused primarily on the rugby-sized thighs of the

man squatting in the hot corner.

The innings moved along. Mickey talked, ordered a hot dog, got

up and yelled something down into the dugout and laughed afterwards.

Mickey watched. Mickey held court. All the while, Sonny was thinking

about the night. About how he would target Vinnie, how he would

separate him from Mickey, how it would go, how the getaway might go.

And all of a sudden, though he swatted the thought aside, it seemed

rushed. All of it. How could he expect to get it done, done well and

without attention, tonight? And get Katie out of Los Angeles *and* drop

the car if necessary *and* see the Cuban girl? He had forgotten her name momentarily in his confusion and thus her order of priority firmly established by circumstance.

He knew that he had to piss, he also knew that he had to stand, to get out and walk the Gilmore Field concessions. To clear his head if only for a few moments.

Sonny leaned towards Katie, and whispered, "Be back soon." He squeezed her hand briefly as he departed.

***

Katie watched the game, at once bored and entertained, like following baseball is wont to be. Sonny had been gone only a minute or two when the big mobster, the tall fat one who looked like he came from a mobster catalog, walked up the stairs, the same direction Sonny had gone. She considered briefly following both of them that direction to tell Sonny, if she found him first. She also considered that his anger at returning and not finding her minding the situation outweighed even the best possibilities of a wild goose chase searching for him. She would sit, watch the game, and tell him about it upon his return. She nodded at her decision as though it had been confirmed by another.

***

Sonny stood at the trough in the bathroom, pissing out his dailies. He had a hand against the wall, a rather common habit judging by the amount of fingerprints into the white paint, at once singular and cooperative. This pissing thing was not as easy as it was when he was younger. The urge was the same. The process, not so much.

As he began zipping up, a tall man shouldered him without grace and positioned himself. Sonny looked up reflexively and immediately recognized the man as Big Vinnie. He was surprised to find that his first reaction was to gut him there where he stood, this man who had told him of his wife's infidelity, to finish this wicked night, walk Katie to the car and be done with it. But he quickly looked around at the approximate dozen men in the bathroom and recognized the impossibility of such a thought. The risk, given such things. He intuitively pulled his hat low onto his brow ridges and turned his back. A man tapped his shoulder; he ignored it.

"Hey buddy," said a voice behind him.

Sonny ignored it.

"Buddy!" the voice repeated.

Sonny turned, and in doing so realized something then that he didn't much like in himself. He realized then that he *wanted* Vinnie to see him, wanted the recognition and meaningless sense of power that accompanied it.

Vinnie looked at him and said, "I just wanted to apologize for clippin you like that. I mean—," he stopped there. His eyes began some process of understanding, despite the purple eye and camouflaging of ink and the stain of years.

"Hey! We knew you was—" was what Vinnie was able to get out next, as he raised his finger and pointed to Sonny.

Sonny was on him then, pushing him backwards, pounding the midsection, then atop him as they fell bakwards. He had grabbed the outstretched finger and felt the bone give upon his reckless charge. Once on the ground, he connected solidly to the face, twice, as the big man bucked beneath him. Most of his punches had fallen without mark, as the frantic moment passed from something of enjoyment to something separate entire. Sonny fumbled then into his back pocket and fingered there a knife and slid it open and punched quickly into the groin. And again. He felt the men grabbing his arms and lifting him off his target, saw his enemy beneath him begin to set himself anew, an attempt to get his bearings and begin to stand. Vinnie's mouth manipulated into an O without sound. The bloodletting had engulfed his pantleg and he stumbled backwards and shook slightly upon recognizing the source of his discomfort. The big man reached down and touched the invasive and protruding handle softly but did not pull on it. As if it simply should not be there. Sonny recognized the danger of the moment and in it saw only the panic of the animal.

He kicked backwards twice and threw his head as a weapon and found that the arms that held his had let go. Sonny surged forward and escaped the grasping hands. He ran for the exit and used the corner as a fulcrum to expedite his departure. He ran breathlessly to the section and then the row and walked with his hat low to Katie and nodded for her to go and left through the opposite side of the row he had begun, much to the chagrin of those seated there. He could see that his hands were spotted in blood. He could see there was a commotion near the bathroom as he glanced in that direction, and grabbed Katie's tiny bicep and led her opposite as if time were theory only and could be manipulated by will alone.

Upon reaching the car, Sonny turned and looked back towards the field and the haze of lights fighting back the darkness, little candles against the allover black. It was a look that held disappointment and adrenaline and an anguish that was palpable and had a pulse. He saw that no one had followed them. Yet. That they were unburdened by the night. Momentarily free, despite simple mathematics. He looked across the roof of the merc and there Katie's eyes back at him. He saw confusion there, but also sympathy, and at that he wiped his hand across the whole of his face and opened the car door and seated himself. He opened the passenger door as well and she sat and stared at him and said nothing. The blood on his hands had dried and stained the skin there like ink. The engine throttled to life again, the silence broken by rhythm.

"I'm gonna drop you with Mick for a bit," he said.

She looked at him and her eyes lengthened and her mouth grew to object.

"I'll pick you up before I go anywhere. *Promise,*" he finished, looked at her, and smiled something painful.

She looked at him still. Said nothing.

"Kid, I practically just made you accessory to what just happened. What am I gonna do, *hide?*"

Katie looked out the windshield as if to cry for a moment before breaking into a sobbing laughter, and said, through pinched cries, "You're obviously not very good at *that!*" Sonny smiled at her bravery and she laughed at his inability to remain out of the shadows. It carried them some distance, and as the lights of Gilmore Field faded from the rearview mirror, Sonny was left to ponder the inadequacies of his present, the chances given those undeserving. He saw the girl look at his hands upon the steering wheel, the stains there. He wondered why he thought his return to Los Angeles would provide her some comfort, and wondered at the ramifications of his life versus hers and the infinite space between.

***

Sonny had hurt enough people in his day. He knew that the wound he had

given the fat man was near fatal. The blood indicated as much. There was

an artery there, in the leg, that was nothing to play with. He couldn't have

named it, but knew its approximate location nonetheless. Ten to fifteen

seconds of injury had bled his pants to the ankle red. He assumed Vince

among the deceased, and saw him shaking and faroff in his mind's eye as he

went. But this victory, regardless of how shallow, how dangerous, how

improvised it had occurred, left Sonny with a smirk upon reflection.

He dropped Katie off at Mick's and drove now to Miryea's, the

name he had forgotten upon recall earlier in the night. He drove there not

to celebrate, but to take in something entirely human, to regain bearings at

once feared lost and without handle. The Merc carried now a doubly

wanted man, a bloodied man, cash and luggage in the trunk and the dented

fender peculiar to its own history. He felt a tophatted wolf just then,

picking his teeth and strutting about the forest. Sonny smoked a cigarette

to the wick of his fingers and grinned in the spring Los Angeles night,

vertical rows of palm trees passing like iron bars along the boundary of the

forbidden.

A TRUNK FULL OF ZEROES

The address given on the slip of paper led him to an area wholly unfamiliar. Once upon a time, Sonny Haynes knew much of Los Angeles like a convert to the given scriptures, knew the alleys and the clubs, both legal and creative, where to score skag on a Friday night without advance notice, where to park for Hollywood Legion Stadium for the fights, knew every bouncer who worked the Olympic Auditorium and had the shortcuts to the morgue by rote. Now he simply felt a tourist. This was not his city anymore but a facsimile given coincidence. Like the childhood room in the elderly parent's house. It all looked familiar, but it was not his anymore.

Sonny eased the Merc into a spot between a Cadillac sedan and a truck across the street from the address he had been given. The streetlamps pooled onto the concrete in lighted circles and the palm trees bent gently in the wind. The iconic rustle. Sonny looked the street down and saw nothing of concern from his vantage, but that admittedly was one without the benefit of light or geographical knowledge.

In other words, Sonny thought, I might as well be blind as a fortuneteller and naïve as a newborn for all I know about being here. About what waits for me behind that door. There were second thoughts to be had then, ideas of leaving without saying goodbye, ideas of not sticking with something even when that something is without the promise of return, ideas that other men have. He contemplated those thoughts for a moment and left them behind like a dream unremembered. A car drove past and there the fickle headlight upon the dashboard, his bloodstained hands resting on the steering wheel. He spit on his hands then, rubbing them one to another in an effort to remove the given stains, and then he exited the car and walked the concrete down, his heels clicking softly on the gravel, any concern about the fortunes of a man from tonight until tomorrow forgotten. The present was what it was, Sonny figured, and tomorrow owed no promises anyways.

Miryea lived in the rear portion of a duplex just off Ocean Park. The structure bled Los Angeles, from its concrete pathways to the Spanish stucco walls and the tiled rooftop. Sonny looked at the front door, darkened and outfitted with plants, cacti and the like. Things difficult even to death. He continued along the walkway to the rear door. The rooms unlit and awash in darkness throughout the unit. He checked his watch, angling it towards the front porch light, which read but 10:12 pm. Late, but late enough for every light in the house to be out? Sonny thought nothing on it, then tried the front door. It opened like something on a swivel. Like something that swung to and fro like a gate. He fingered the lock and there the splinters bashed asunder without the metal coupling. The door had been kicked in. Sonny's stomach dropped like a two-seater on a roller coaster.

He had no flashlight and cursed himself once for feeling unprepared and yet again without forethought. As he opened the front door, the night stars and small porch light provided little illumination on the hardwood floors. He found a light switch upon the wall and flicked it topmost. With the light appeared three door frames and two feet splayed awkwardly in the centermost. Sonny pulled the .45 from his pants and breathed slowly, focused on the sound of his footfalls. He figured he knew whose feet were vertical. He would verify them last. He walked the hallways slowly in the dark, gun drawn, to silence amid the cathedral of night. Room to room the flat was empty. Full only of darkness and the detritus of everyday. Wire hangers and a towel hanging from the shower rod. He returned to the living room and there the feet askew like some unanswered question. One shoe had been thrown, the other lay hanging by the brown toes as if she were in the process of flipping it askance while minding the ritual of something meaningless, placing the keys in their bowl or opening the mail.

Sonny slowly walked to the doorframe before looking down. Miryea lay still in a flowered sundress upon the linoleum of the kitchen. Her eyes were closed and she looked asleep except for the jagged fenceline upon her neck, bruised throughout and bloodclotted in spots. Sonny knelt down to touch her and placed fingers to neck, not so much to check for a pulse but for a sense of something human. There was nothing to it; she had begun to cool already and felt heavy and assembled of a rubber skin. The poetry of possibility was lost, then. He brought his hand to his face in an impulse built of instinct not yet gone, some practice in uniformity to the human race. He rubbed his face hastily and looked down again.

Still Miryea, still dead.

Sonny knew the ramifications here before they were explained to him. Knew that this was his fault. Knew that his appearance into this girl's life had brought about a reckoning without absolution. Knew that she was without blame. He knew also that he needed to get out before others came. So he could get to New Orleans, protect Katie. Another stone bruise to the soul without judgment.

Using his handkerchief as a duster, Sonny called the police hotline and left them the address, anonymously. He hung up the phone and wiped down the doorknobs, light switches, and Miryea. Washed his hands in the bathroom sink, and wiped that down. Then he knelt by the body of the Cuban woman and said something then, him to her, that has since been forgotten. He walked out to his car with his gun drawn. The crickets sang the Los Angeles night down and the darkness, as it is wont to do, offered absence alone.

Sonny started up the Merc and merged into onto the blacktop. He navigated that way for some time, letting circumstance and the car be the driver, staying in the relative dark and on side streets until he passed the parking lot of a liquor store. The Hi-Hat. The neon lit the stars above with a drum kit complete with blinking cymbals. There was no forethought at all upon parking the car in the lot and walking in. Sonny

could hardly have retraced the steps that put him there. He found himself

buying a bottle of Four Roses and sat in his car again.

He stared out the window as he twisted the lid from its bearings.

Without hesitation he brought the bottle to his nose and there the burnt

caramel and charcoal and a short heat. He sucked it down then in

voluminous gasps, the burn palpable and something of worth. The whiskey

went down like a medicine at once curing illness and beginning another.

Upon quenching whatever thirst that particular demon demanded, he took

the bottle from his lips and examined it, as if reading the label. One third of

the fifth was empty, the contents either burning in Sonny's innards or left

in stained rivulets about his mouth and neck. He opened the car door and

walked to the entrance of the liquor store and knelt as in prayer to leave

the bottle there outside the door, lidless & mostly full. Some gift for the

night and what would receive it.

In his car, he leaned back in the seat and sighed deeply. The liquor

filled him with a terrible fire that shamed him like some memory that

would not shake free. He sobbed once, at something without reckoning,

and pounded the heel of his right hand against the steering wheel three

times as if it had been the conduit through which his misery found voice.

When he had finished, he rested his head against the large steering wheel

and let it lay until he could breathe again.

A TRUNK FULL OF ZEROES

***

He arrived at Mick's after midnight. He parked the car in back and walked the alley as if he were lighter by twenty pounds and ten years. He recognized the buzz from years ago, knew that it was only a mask for what lay beneath. But it also brought with it a sense of freedom and a singing contentment that the gods could not deny. He hoped that nobody would notice. He hoped that his failures would remain his alone.

Ray was at the backdoor and allowed Sonny entrance, all glinting teeth and toothpick in the alley light. Sonny footed the dark hallway and stopped in the restroom to relieve himself and wash his neck and chin free of the stench of liquor. The restroom was free of accoutrements. As if Mick had run out of finance before the restroom had been built. As if the relieving of one's bladder deserved nothing more than the necessary. It offered a toilet and a urinal and the porcelain throughout grimed and rimmed in brown lines. The mirror was broken in the leftmost corner and warped and scratched allover so that the reflection offered in return to a given glance was like a jigsaw puzzle unable to form anew. The self, unrecognizable. Sonny dried his hands on the soiled towel and walked through the red beads and there a roomful of patrons, the static of conversation at once garbled and anonymous. The everyday conversation you never have. He immediately saw Mick behind the bar tending customers and scanned the room once. Katie was in the corner sitting by herself, the table cluttered with a book and a deck of cards attendant like a stuffed animal discarded. She smiled and waved when she saw him and Sonny smirked and nodded once in reply.

He slid across the red plastic seating in the booth, and the two of them looked at one another each to each. Though he had just held the hand of a woman who would have held his in return had she been anything but dead, and though he had run through the innards of Los Angeles like a man on fire since his homecoming and taken advantage of the city and its citizens like a spoiled child on his birthday, Sonny smiled at Katie as if for the first time. Teeth showing and face creased like a grimace with a purpled baby eggplant growth in his eyesocket. Here was something from his past worth hanging onto, and things on that side of the ledger were few indeed at present. She smiled back, though hers was more in response than initiation.

"You ready to blow this city out?" Sonny asked. "We got places to go, kid."

Katie looked at him, her expression all locked closets and lost infancy. Then looked down at the deck of cards as if an answer were writ there.

"We got a long friggin drive," he bulled forward. "Go down south for a spell," Sonny said, trying to be upbeat. To ignore what he should not. He hoped she wasn't smelling the liquor on his breath. He couldn't tell and it ate at the moment.

"You killed a man tonight, didn't you? At the field?" Katie asked. The questions were hours late but no less pertinent for the continuation of the night. For everything of worth. She looked at his face as she asked him as if the truth were something tangible to be read like print.

Sonny looked back at her without answer. He studied his hands as if they had not been cleaned. As if the evidence still stained the skin there. He wondered at the harm in truth. He thought of the blood on his hands, the lies available to them. Then: "*Yeah*," he croaked. "I did. The big Italian guy. He—," Sonny stopped then and sniffed and looked Katie in the eyes. "Yeah. I did," he said, and finished by nodding once.

"*Because* he hurt Betty," Katie said, not as a question, but as a statement that needed confirmation.

"Yeah," Sonny said, and stayed silent thereafter. He nodded then like a bobblehead in a land of speed bumps.

"You gonna hurt more people?" Katie asked, her innocence displayed without the benefit of its appearance.

Sonny smiled then. "Well," he said, "that depends on just who they try to hurt around *me*." He cracked his knuckles as he finished in what he hoped would pass for levity.

Katie smiled at that and reached out and hugged Sonny like he were the world's biggest teddy bear. As if he was responsible only for the benign dependencies of the world.

Mick stood above them then. Both of them unaware as to how long he had been there. When Katie separated her embrace from Sonny, they all looked at one another, each to each without word.

Finally, Mick broke the silence with a whisper: "So you've come to drop somethin off for me?"

"I already left it in your toilet," Sonny remarked.

"Eeeeewwww," Katie moaned, and slapped Sonny on the shoulder.

"Dropped an Irishman in there, didya?" Mick answered, and cowed the room with the laugh that attended it.

As the moment died, Sonny looked back at Mick with response to his original question and nodded.

"You'll be leavin for a bit?"

"'Fraid so," Sonny confirmed.

Mick halted in thought. The room seemed in wait. Finally: "D'ya think anybody might be askin your whereabouts, then?"

"I've never been to the South," Katie said to nobody in particular.

"I'll find you a game somewhere," Sonny said. "Keep you busy." He then looked back up at Mick, looming over them unkempt like some brigand born in the wrong century. "I'd hope not," he continued, this time to Mick. "What would they ask you my whereabouts for? Haven't seen each other in years."

"My thoughts exactly. It's like askin' a Scotsman for a loan. A paradox from the fuckin start. He can't give ya none if there's no money to start from. Say goodbye, the both of ya, before ya leave, yeah?" He looked at Sonny as he said it, slapped the table softly once without explanation, and turned back to his red establishment, which hummed in rhythm with the night.

Sonny walked to the Merc in back and made sure the necessaries were in order. All the while the nagging revelations of the evening hung about him like whisper. He knew that the only person to whom he had mentioned Miryea was Harold, and the thought that his old partner had informed on him made his short hairs bristle. He would think of other angles, attempt to connect the dots in ways peculiar to normal thought, but the coincidence of the thing would never leave. And if Miryea, then H had called the hit on him the first time. Outside the diner. And what did H know of Betty then? Well. He would deal those possibilities upon his return. He shook his head at the surprise of it all, at the neverending failures of everyone close to him, and he did not exclude himself from that group.

Sonny moved much of Sanchez's money from the trunk into the corners of his bag and hid the rest in a small storage compartment under a blanket. Katie had two bags as well, and he would have rather she trimmed it to one, but would let that go. Some concessions were necessary for the civility of the thing, he figured. Hank's leather bag—also full of cash—leaned against the rear of the thing. An obscene amount of bills for a normal man and his not-daughter to be transporting on a crosscountry trip without reason. He sighed. The click of Ray's footfalls shortened the alley until he stood next to Sonny looking in the trunk as well. Ray was smoking a brown cigarette and had his hat tilted back so far on his head it seemed held there by some unseen hand.

"You ready, then?" He asked.

Sonny took out a cigarette and set flame to it against the night. He nodded at the question and closed the trunk.

***

It was early morning when Sonny and Katie rode east in the dark womb of the Merc out of Los Angeles. He saw a sign for San Diego on the 6 south and asked Katie if she had ever been. Then he began talking. He didn't even wait for her answer. His last trip there had been a day excursion to San Diego with Betty some years prior. He thought for a moment of the year and realized that it made no difference now. It was dead history, no matter how many times he replayed the failing memory. The San Diego Zoo, he recalled. That had been a part of it. The lion had tried to jump the moat when a flash bulb had gone off. Fragments. The majesty of the neck of a giraffe. These are things I hold onto, he thought. It all comes down to this, these small nothings remade into a life. He shook his head and tried to rid the fractured thoughts that resonated like the chorus of a pop song embedded in the psyche. He looked at her then, completely unaware as to what had been spoken as opposed to thought. She wore the look of the sympathetic, looking up at him with a slightly scrunched brow and pursed lips.

"I know you miss her, Sonny. It's—It's just all over you," she said, and lay her hand on his shoulder in sympathy. It was all she knew how to say and felt remiss for not knowing more. He nodded, once, and forced his gaze to the road.

There were few cars out at this time, and once they left Los Angeles proper, fewer still. Within a half hour, Katie was asleep and soundless in her slumber. Sonny had no intention whatsoever of stopping until they arrived in New Orleans, but of course that was impossible. Texas, now that was a possibility. He smiled at the possibility.

A TRUNK FULL OF ZEROES

The 99 east carried them through the remainder of Los Angeles
County. There was little to see along the two-lane road besides the
darkness and the hypnotic repetition of equally stunted lines on the
pavement. Movies make road trips look fun. In reality, they are endurance
tests of the senses, surrounded by tedium. There was nothing on the radio
but static this late at night. He considered listening to that. There were
stretches where the two-lane road was being made into four what for all
the cars expected in the Southern California area in the coming years.
Construction signs where Sonny could see none of the construction in the
lack of light. Along the road, he passed San Bernardino, which he knew to
be originally a Mormon settlement, then Redlands, known throughout
California for its oranges. And eventually, the San Gorgonio Pass, all
12,000 feet of its peak invisisble in the darkness. He looked over at Katie
then, who rubbed the side of her head and readjusted herself from one
uncomfortable resting place to another. Her bobbed hair stuck out at
precarious angles and her face seemed without loss. Sonny lit a Chesterfield
and smoked the night down.

He wondered how he had gotten to this point from his origins.
The widower of a wife and a suspect in her murder, a former cop turned
muscle, now watchdog for this 16-year old girl who represented anything
that once mattered. He looked over the ink that stained his arms in the

carlight. The raised skin, alien to his birth. And here he was, returning to the region he swore he'd never. Such things. He decided then that he would stop and see Del, damn the consequences. One segway along the way to New Orleans. He thumped the steering wheel once in confirmation and rolled the window down halfway, smelling the night like it was something tangible and free.

***

The sun rose red along the crested rocks below the eastern sky as he parked in the lot of a truck stop. The Merc needed gas. He needed to eat. And piss. It was one-stop shopping for the folks from the coast. He intentionally jerked to a stop and Katie slid forward on the seat and off of it entirely, softly slamming once onto the dashboard and was sitting up almost immediately.

"Wha-," she managed to croak and shook her head like a swivel. Then she looked at Sonny and he with a smile though he tried otherwise and she smacked him on the arm, hard, and fell back against the seat.

"Rise and shine, darlin. We are just west of Phoenix, Arizona, and in need of replenishment." He hatted himself and stepped out of the car.

The truck stop was a large brick building, square and squat, with a couple of windows. There was a sign, elevated and singular in letter, announcing that it was a TRUCK STOP, anchored outside the building. The parking lot had about two-hands worth of rig's, and besides that there were a few sedans, mostly Ford's, scattered about like a child's toys next to the trucks. He swung the doors open to the coffee shop portion of the establishment and waited for Katie. There was a *Please Wait To Be Seated* sign and a lady sitting on a stool behind a cash register next to it. She had glasses on that were bejeweled in the uppermost portion and a hairdo that just kept going up.

"You need some breakfast, honey?"

"Yeah. What's the specialty of the house?" He smiled at her.

She looked at him like he had asked her the combining elements involved in the atom bomb. A problem unsolvable. Seconds passed. Neither of them moved, and the awkwardness was sewn into the moment like an illfitting coat. Then, as if it had been perched on the tip of her tongue all along, she answered, "The hash is the best, you ask me."

"I just did," Sonny said.

"Yep. Nice shiner you got there. Looks like you're growin a vegetable on your face." She cackled at her own joke.

He stood there in the lobby, waiting. Looked out the window and saw that Katie had finally exited the car and was walking towards the diner.

"You ever gonna want a seat, or is your thing just waitin in the waitin section?," she asked. Sonny looked at her with lots to say and said none of it. He looked instead at her fingers to see if a man at home was subjected to this as well. He was.

Finally, Katie walked in through the doorway and stood at his side. They made eye contact and smiled one to another, her eyes closing in mock exaggeration. The cobwebs of night had been shaken and the Arizona morning was getting to its feet outside.

"So are we ready yet, or are there more surprises still comin?," the waitress again. Sonny had forgotten about her.

"Yeah," he said. "A booth. Over there," and he pointed to a window seat where he could see the car.

She rolled her eyes at the request and grabbed the menus from their holder.

***

The food tasted like truck stop food should taste. It was hot, and it was breakfast. The eggs were overcooked and rubbery, the toast nearly cold by the time it arrived, the bacon could have gotten up and ran away it was so undercooked. But the two of them were so famished that they noticed all of it and said nothing and instead shoveled it down like it was their last meal. Sonny hoped that it wouldn't be.

When they had nearly finished the process, and pushed their plates into the middle of the table, and wiped their greasy mouths with napkins, only then did they set about to talking.

"So," Katie started. "Where are we going, what are we doing? I mean, down South, New Orleans, sure, but, y'know. And I'm sure you've got some *instructions,* or rules for me, right?"

"Yeah. I do," Sonny said, and looked back at his plate as if he held hopes it had been refilled.

She rolled her eyes at him, the second time a female had rolled their eyes at him this morning, and here it was still before 7am. But Katie did it playfully, as if a game were beginning and she knew the rules better than he did. He didn't doubt that for a second.

"We're headed down New Orleans way, Sonny said. "Got a package to drop for a couple of people that aren't expecting it."

She nodded.

"I figure we'll stop somewhere in New Mexico or Texas tonight, hole up in a motel. Then tomorrow we're makin' a detour. Gonna stop outside of El Paso at an old buddy's place. Del. You may have heard Betty and I mention him."

She gave no indication that this was the case, but he continued nonetheless.

"Maybe stay the night there. I could use some of that old man's sarcasm," he said, and looked out the window. "Then we'll head a straight shot through Texas to New Orleans. Now that's what we're doin. As for the *rules*," and he mock rolled his eyes to mimic hers and in doing so felt a sharp pain in his eggplant eye. He pointed to the car, then looked about them to make sure his words were theirs alone, and lowered his voice. "We've got a lot of cash in the trunk of that car. You got me?"

She nodded again, listening actively. He was happy with that. It's tough to get a teenager to listen to anything, but she was engaged. She needed to be.

"Now normally," he continued, "I might not even tell you that. But I need you keeping an eye out for us now too. You see anybody near that car and you get me on the run. Yeah?"

"Got it, Sarge." She mock saluted him, but he could tell there was comprehension behind it.

"Another thing," he said. "We need to avoid cops. Any cops. You see 'em, you linger for a moment or two and casually make yourself scarce. If we get stopped on the road, well, that could be trouble. And I aint gonna run from them. I'll just pull over, casual as can be, and be polite until I can't be anymore. As for you, you're my daughter." He paused a moment to look out at the car, and continued: "No reason to run from 'em, that'll just be a bigger mess. I gotta tell you all this just in case. Hopefully in two days time we're in New Orleans and none of it matters." He looked away, towards the kitchen, uncomfortable telling her things he was sorry to have even involved her in.

As he looked away, she spoke. "Sonny," she said. "It's gonna be alright. I know it is. I don't know how, I just know. Like I knew mom wasn't coming home. We'll be ok." She smiled then, as out of place as whiskey in church, and said: "You'll see."

He looked at her and nodded, unaware as to how somebody so unprepared for the possible consequences could be sure of anything. Ultimately, he loved her attitude and spunk, but he also knew that her confidence came first from youth, and moreso from her belief in him. And that was the most uncomfortable realization of all.

He went to the bathroom and when he came out Katie was looking at quarter books on the spinner. Mostly pulp and thriller fiction. Trash fiction, they called it. "They got any Chandler?" he asked.

"Don't see any," she said. "Lotsa westerns."

"Pick something out, if you want it," he said, and walked over to the counter.

The man there was very fat and oily with a creased neck that held numerous small moles that looked like tiny raisins and he smelled of pickles, and Sonny hated the smell of pickles, which reminded him of his youth. Growing up in Tennessee, his father pickled everything possible and the jars still lay about the ledges in Sonny's memory larger than actuality. There was a jar of pickles next to jar of pickled eggs on the counter. He nearly gagged.

Katie chose a Jim Thompson book, *Nothing More Than Murder*, and a pack of gum. The fat man leered at her when she approached the counter as some men are wont to do. Sonny noticed it but recognized it only as a desperate want without handle, and in it a mixture of resentment and sympathy.

***

Once more on the road, Sonny smoking and Katie rolling the radio dial to find something besides static. She found a Country-Western station and on it played *Long Gone Lonesome Blues* by Hank Williams with His Drifting Cowboys.

She had started in on her book and leaned against the passenger door.

"I got a question for you, kiddo."

She looked up, annoyed for a brief moment for the break in concentration, and then caught his eyes as participant.

"I'm worried about school for you. You don't go to school, like most kids your age would be, *should* be, so I'm worried about what you're gonna do when you get older," he said.

She tilted her head to the side, and asked, "What do you mean?"

"I mean, for a job. Y'know, a livelihood. I mean, I know you're only 16, don't get me wrong, but, well, most people get diploma's and such."

She chuckled once at him and his attempt. "Don't be silly, Sonny. Why would I need a job? I can make money anytime I want with poker." She shook her head at his lack of understanding of the simple things.

He knuckled the steering wheel and bit his tongue. He had forgotten that it was not a hobby she had, but a gift. She needed a caretaker, perhaps a father figure, but a paycheck was not the issue, and probably never would be. He wanted to say that gambling was no way to make a living, wanted to say that those things can't be relied upon, wanted to say lots of things that would come out sounding self-righteous and outright silly. How was he one to give advice? Carrying a 16-year old across the country running from a murder rap and with a trunk full of cash?

Yeah, that's rich, he thought. Gamble away, doll. Gamble away.

16.

The 390 miles separating Phoenix and Las Cruces was a stretch of sorts that reminded Sonny of Mexico. Rock assemblages running from red to yellow and the striations lined within. Clearly God's work and if not the god of scripture then the god of nature. But some god set his hand upon this land in the ancient and had kept it the same ever since. At least that's how Sonny figured it. Thunderheads gathered east on the skyline ominous as silence. He wondered if they'd travel far enough to find them.

The trip on the two-lane interstate was a slow one as truck after truck paused their progress, but the stretches of open road were ecstatic in their freedom. The two travelers drove with the windows down and the wind whipping about the cabin like a dervish. Sonny had his snapcap on and Katie's hair was held in a headband to allow her the necessary vision to read. They had found another Country-Western station, and the radio blared steel guitar and fiddle barely audible above the wind. The air was heavy with the approach of humidity that the stormclouds brought forth.

Sonny looked over at Katie absorbed in her book more than once and thought that if the fragility and flaws of life glimpsed perfection only in small moments, this might indeed be one of them.

As the sun reached its apex and then began its slow descent, before hiding entirely behind the coming sky, Sonny stopped the Merc in Lordsburg for a meal. Upon entering the town, it was clear that not much went on here. In fact, probably not much had gone on since its inception in 1880, started as it was by the Western Pacific railroad line, and the scar of track and rail ran directly through the town. The sign upon entering said that it was a waypoint for travelers, and Sonny didn't imagine it had ever been anything else. Nonetheless, they found a café on what seemed to be the only street with any businesses open and stopped there. There were clusters of dried chili peppers hanging from the rafters and the waitress was a Mexican woman who spoke little and smiled often.

***

They were eating cheeseburgers and talking about the book she had bought when a youthful-looking priest walked in and sat in the booth next to theirs. He ordered a cup of coffee and looked over at the two of them.

"Say, that your Mercury out there?" he asked.

Sonny looked at him and said nothing. Could be this was trouble. Could be that the father is an admirer of cars. Could be that he would have to bloody up a priest. Katie stared at Sonny and the priest stared and Sonny and these things all ran through his head in a second while he stared back, not answering.

"Well, if it is, that is one heckuva vehicle. Gorgeous," said the priest.

"Gets us from place to place," Sonny said, at long last, before fingering some steak fries into his mouth.

"Place to place!," the priest guffawed. "I'll bet that thing cruises like nothing at all. Why, I've thought about getting one myself, but I don't think those in my parish would very well like their priest driving around in a car quite so—," and there he stopped, thinking of the word.

"*Violent,*" Sonny said. Helping the conversation along.

The priest scrunched his face. "Well, no," he said. "I wasn't going to say that. But, well—so *visceral,*" he said. Pleased with the word. "Visceral," he repeated. "No, don't think that it'd be very proper."

"Does that matter?" Katie asked, genuinely interested.

"Oh, I think it matters very much, young lady," he answered. "Our flock looks to me to show them the way, to lead by example. No, it wouldn't do to drive around in one of those." He smiled. "But that doesn't mean I don't like to take a look."

"I see," she said. "You think it'd be hypocritical."

The priest thought that one over. "In a way, yes," he said after some introspection. "So, I saw the plates from California. You just visiting from over that way?" His question held no hint of malice, nothing besides a man of the cloth being friendly with strangers in the town, but it was all Sonny could do not to react poorly. He took a deep breath and wondered what he had done to deserve having to threaten a priest.

Then Katie answered: "Well, my dad here's got an old Army buddy down below Palomas and said he had run into a great deal with a dealer out of El Paso on a few Mercury sedans." The priest was nodding with understanding. "You see," she continued, "he had to get rid of the old models, 'cept he was gonna ship 'em into Mexico, to a dealer outside Juarez who could still sell them on account of it being Mexico and all. So, dad and his buddy each bought one for more than the Mexican dealer was gonna give 'em but for way less than than they are up here in America—and they get run through California, so the plates are the real deal." She winked at the priest then. "You should look into it sometime. Best way to get a deal. So anyways, we figured we'd see some of the country is all, y'know?"

The priest answered: "Yes, maybe I will look into it. That sounds like something, all right."

Sonny stared at his little pupil in awe. Then he said: "Alright, Padre. We gotta hit the road. But you take care now." He stood from the table and Katie with him.

He paid at the register and Katie waved to the priest, still sipping his coffee before they walked out the door and into the day that was darkening down in a hurry.

***

Once again on the 70 east and outside the town limits of Lordsburg, New Mexico, Sonny turned to Katie, and said, "Whoa. Where'd you come up with that?"

She smiled and fluttered her eyelashes at him. "Do I have to tell you all my little secrets, big man?," she answered, as not so much an answer as a tease.

"Fine. But what was the best thing you did," he asked, in lieu of a quiz.

"Ummm, well. Let's see. I kept you from answering with a threat and leaving him either physically hurt of just more suspicious, I kept him off guard by me answering to begin with, and my answer involved three different city names to keep the whole thing as confusing as possible. Is that about right?" She asked, already knowing the answer.

He shook his head. "Smartass," he said, but not without a hint of pride.

Sonny wanted to make Texas tonight. He figured that they might even be able to make Del's, possibly. But a storm was definitely coming in, and he was tired. Bonetired. It had been days since he had slept and driving tired at night and in the rain when he couldn't be pulled over for any reason sounded about as smart as killing a man in a packed baseball stadium and believing that nobody would see you. So, caution being Sonny's middle name, he decided that they would call it a night in Las Cruces.

The rain had already started falling in the city limits when they arrived. They were big drops blotting the windshield and when Sonny put his hand outside the window, they carried with them a warmth more typical of the South than the Southwest.

The motel was named the Wagon Wheel. Sonny always stayed at a motel called the Wagon Wheel when possible. It was one of his quirks. And in this region, there were plenty of such possibilities. He paid for a room with cash and used a name that was not his and claimed that he did not have his ID. The clerk was reading the newspaper throughout and seemed entirely unconcerned. He dropped the paper low enough to see that the money was there and the form filled, and returned to his reading.

Sonny backed the car into the spot directly in front of the room.

The room was adorned in everything cowboy. Rooms in motels named the

Wagon Wheel generally were. The carpets were a mélange of brown and

yellow. The bedspreads had drawings from a rodeo on them, and the table

was literally a wagon wheel with a glass top. The lamp had a covered

wagon at its base and its pulls were horseshoes. Very coordinated, those

designers, Sonny thought.

When Katie walked in with her bag, she stopped in the doorway

and said, Wow.

"Yeah, they don't spare the cowboy design, do they?" Sonny said,

smiling at her reaction.

"Yikes."

"It won't hurt ya. It's only one night."

She dropped her bag on her bed and immediately stretched out

across the whole of it.

***

They each showered and lay on their beds and talked little. The exhaustion

of the last few days had set in, but Sonny knew that she would want some

privacy, some private time after spending nearly the last 48 hours by his side. He certainly would have wanted that at her age. He sat up on his bed.

"Hey. I'm gonna head to the bar for a bit. Get some coffee. Let you relax some. Do your girl stuff. Or whatever."

She smiled at his awkwardness. "Alright," she said. "I don't know that I need any, but that's very gentlemanly of you."

"If anybody knocks at the door," Sonny said, "you don't answer, doesn't matter who they are. Got it? And if you need something, come over there, but be sure to lock the door behind you."

"K. I'm kinda hungry. Bring something back, would you?"

"You got it, kiddo," he said, as he put a collared shirt on over his wifebeater and footed his brogues and attached his hat. "I'll be back in maybe an hour," he said. She stood from the bed and hugged him around the trunk before letting go and reseating herself.

"Thanks," she said.

"For what?" he asked.

"For keeping us safe."

He chuckled at her naivete. "Well," he said. "I don't know that we are *safe*, but I'm not gonna let anybody hurt you. Ok?"

"Oh. Kay," she said, and nodded the two syllables individual and distinct as he walked out the door and into the falling rain, careful to make sure it locked behind him.

***

The bar was a bit like a cavern. It was just off the lobby, and Sonny took

pains to avoid walking by the windows. He figured it safe to avoid the gaze

of the clerk who had ignored him the first time—no reason to give second

chances at a time like this. The walls were rocklike and jagged, and the

carpet stained and red. To nobody's surprise, the tables were wagon

wheels and the chairbacks made to look the same. There were western

paintings on the walls, Remington knockoffs mostly, and an old Winchester

rifle hanging above the bar.

The jukebox in the corner played *You Broke Your Promise* by

Louis Jordan and the barkeep was working on a crossword. There was a

couple in the corner drinking red wine and two men at the other end of the

bar. Sonny took a stool.

"What can I get you?" The barkeep asked, without moving.

"Some coffee would be great," Sonny answered, and lit a

Chesterfield.

With that, the man looked up. "Coffee? Let me check on that."

He walked over to the pot, smelled it, and scrunched his nose. "Gotta make

a fresh pot," he said. "That okay?"

"I'd rather that anyways. I got time."

"Tell me about it," the bartender said. "Don't we all. Where you from?"

"Tennessee, originally. Then here and there."

"The volunteer state. Very nice. I got some family there. Don't see'm but once in a blue moon, but they's kin nonetheless."

Sonny looked closely at the bartender now and saw him to be a big man. Heavy drinker, judging from the face. Nose flowered with blood vessels in spots, face a bit too big for the head. His hair was gray from the temples up and he was maybe twenty pounds overweight. He seemed kind though, and Sonny couldn't have explained why.

"Well. I got family there too but I've been gone so long the devil lost my name. I'm sure they have too," Sonny answered.

"That's one way to put it. Kin is funny 'cause half the time you don't like 'em but they don't never go nowhere. They always are what they are. Friends, the ones you actually like, they come and go. Don't make a lot of sense, you ask me," he said.

"True enough, I think. So what's what in Las Cruces?" Sonny asked.

"Ummm. Well, there's Mesilla, course, then people go down to the river, do some boatin and things. And there's the University."

"What's Mesilla?"

"It's a small part of the town in the city," he said, as he bent down beneath the counter. "It's the old west portion. Back in them days there were saloons and whorehouses and dancing and theater. And then there's the original building where Billy the Kid was sentenced to hang. He escaped, 'course, but it's got all the signs and such."

"Huh. Well alright," Sonny said, and thought of what Katie might like to do.

"Hey look. I just checked my mugs and I aint got a clean one out here. Gotta go in back and get one. Be back in a coupla minutes." He looked down at the two men at the end of the bar, who were absorbed in conversation and sitting close enough to whisper. "Hey, you guys need anything? I gotta go in back for a minute."

One of the men looked up and said: "No. We're fine." And went back to his conversation as the barkeep left.

Sonny noticed a package of salted peanuts on the counter and pulled it towards him to bring back to the room.

"Hey!" The guy from the end of the bar said. "You gonna pay for that?"

Sonny just looked at him and raised his brows, incredulous. "*Excuse me*," he said, after some seconds.

"I'm just jokin, friend. No need to break my balls." He put his hands up in a mock display of defeat.

The man doing the talking was a small man in stature with curly hair and a flannel shirt on. He walked over to Sonny and sat. "So look," he said, in a voice just above a whisper. "Me and my friend here, we got a job set up tomorrow and our 3rd guy just backed out. Says he got scared or whatever. Anyways, we need a guy. It's an easy gig. And we see you over here with all them tattoos and stuff, well. You been in the joint for a stretch, man? Anyways, it looks like it. You been muscle for somebody, no doubt about that. So I says to my friend over there, I says, here's a guy on our side, and he might just need a job. So what do ya say, friend?"

"No thanks," Sonny answered. There were lots of things he wanted to say, but he figured that sufficed best. He had been holding his tongue lately. He was proud of that. In the kind of way where you stay off red meat for a month and act self-righteous about your sacrifice but really can't wait to gorge yourself on a T-bone when you pass the next steakhouse. That kind of proud.

"Alright, well, you think about it then. Sure could use your car. That sled you got out there in the lot. Whoo boy," he said, and whistled.

"I don't need to think about it," Sonny retorted. "I've got my daughter with me, and we're headed to see family and— "

"Me," the man said, cutting Sonny short, "I've got that Lincoln out there," and he gestured with his thumb to the parking lot.

They both looked out the window and there in the rain sat a 1949 Lincoln Cosmopolitan Town Sedan with suicide doors and a body shape that looked like they had tried making a Mercury and instead ended up with a doublewide bathtub.

"It looks like a bathtub," Sonny said.

"Ahh, see. Now that's just not nice at all, friend," the man said, but followed it with a grin.

"I'm not your friend."

"I see. Well, if you change your mind, friend, lemme know. Fifteen large says you change your mind," and he began walking back to the corner.

Interesting, Sonny thought. I've spent a good portion of my life putting stains like him away and now I look like one of them. Enough so to be offered a job in a public place. He catalogued the thought as the bartender returned with a tray full of clean mugs.

"One hot coffee, coming right up."

"Thanks," Sonny said. "I'll be taking these peanuts too, along with the coffee. And I'll be taking it to go, if it's all the same."

"Whatever works. One cup of coffee to go and one pack of peanuts."

Take Me In Your Arms and Hold Me by Eddy Arnold came on the juke and the steaming mug was put before him. He paid the bartender and nodded to the gentleman in the corner as a gesture of truce. No need making enemies with people who enjoy that role. He sipped his coffee and walked from the cavernous lounge awash in a West that had never quite existed.

***

By the time he keyed open the door and entered, Katie was sound asleep on top of the covers. He put the peanuts on the nightstand and tucked her in. Then he brought all of the bags from the trunk in and put them next to his bed. He didn't like the interest in his car, and didn't need any of that interest to walk away with what was in the trunk while he slept.

He sat propped up in bed drinking his coffee with his .45 on the covers next to him until sleep conquered him as well, and he slept the night through completely and without dream.

17.

The next morning Sonny and Katie packed the car and prepared for Texas. But first, in some fit of what he might later refer to as fatherly instinct, Sonny felt it necessary to show Katie some history. The rain had subsided and the thunderheads had moved westward. So they asked for directions to Mesilla, which ended up being only minutes away, and walked it down. They saw the courtroom where Billy the Kid was sentenced in its original building with the original doors. Not that he was killed there, and not that they held him. But they had prescribed the punishment and thus the papers to prove it. Peppers hung from doorways and the brick and stucco buildings were a testament to another time. Katie smiled from beginning to end and Sonny bought her a postcard of the original Billy the Kid sentencing poster. He found it interesting the fascination with somebody without a shred of decency in them.

Within the hour, they had crossed the Texas border and cruised the 90 east without fanfare. It was a two-lane blacktop through terrain that looked uninhabitable by anything living. Thorny Prickly Pear and flatlands and washes long dried and mountains ever in the distance. Cars were few. Sonny wondered at the reception he would receive from Del. He hadn't seen or talked to the man in more than four years. Just a few months before everything went down in LA. Sonny and Betty had come out here to the ranch and visited Del for nearly a week. They played horseshoes and told stories and went riding and drank margarita's. Just another happy couple visiting an old widower amid the western backdrop. He was surprised how well he remembered that trip. How he and Betty had driven roads much like this one, seemingly still so in love. He shook his head at the thought, at his own foolishness.

It wasn't until the single flashing light went off behind him, however, that he saw things clearly again. A Texas Patrolman was behind him, light on and spinning. Sonny exhaled once in a choke of frustration and pulled over next to a large overhang of rock jutting thirty feet skyward. The patrolman parked behind him and exited. He wore a cowboy hat and sunglasses and a starched khaki uniform. Sonny looked once at Katie and said slowly, "Just go along."

He rolled down his window and the cop leaned in. "License and registration, please," he said.

Sonny responded by giving the man a Mexican ID that Sanchez had made for him years ago. It said his name was William Graves, Sanchez had thought that a funny irony, and included a picture of him from Mexico. The officer looked at it like he had never seen an ID from Mexico or otherwise.

"I don't have the registration papers with me, officer," Sonny explained. "I left them at home. I'll be sure and bring them with me from now on."

The officer looked at the ID, then back at Sonny. "Now that's a shame, aint it, boy? And why exactly do you have an ID from Mexico and a car from California?" The officer must have been a decade Sonny's junior, but used the word nonetheless.

"Don't call me boy, please," Sonny requested. "And yeah, it is too bad. I'll be sure to bring it next time. In fact, it may be in the trunk."

"I beg your pardon, boy. It doesn't seem right for you to be requestin' things from me now, does it?" He paused. "And just where is home, since you claim to be getting on from there?"

The patrolman's radio exploded just then in a static-laden report of an APB. He backed away from the car and spoke to the radio when he was out of earshot. He kept walking to the road and looked both directions. Sonny grabbed the gun and put it in the front of his pants and got out of the car. He looked at Katie quickly, and said, "This could get ugly really quickly. Be careful. If you believe in a god, start prayin."

The patrolman was still on the radio, facing the road, when Sonny unlatched the trunk and opened it. He had planned to look for the registration in the trunk. If the officer showed what came across as hostility or aggression, Sonny would shoot him, put him in his own patrolcar, and drive over into an edged wash and set it on fire. They'd reroute and be in Mexico in an hour. He hoped that didn't happen. You could kill wiseguys sometimes and get away with it. You could kill thugs. You couldn't kill a cop in Texas and be on the lam for long. It could all start unraveling, and quickly. Right here.

The patrolman shouted something into the radio and turned back to Sonny, who had both his hands in the trunk. His left was rummaging while his right straddled the cocked and ready .45.

"Hey!! You get outta there!" The patrolman shouted. "I didn't tell you to get out of the vehicle!" He started walking quickly towards Sonny and reached for his gun.

"I'm just looking for my registration, like you asked," Sonny answered, hoping it would calm the man down—because if it didn't, the man in the cowboy hat was about to die. And Katie was about to be pushed into a life he did not want her to know.

The uniformed man was coming on in big strides, awkwardly attempting to make ground and pull the gun from his buttoned holster.

Here we go, Sonny said to himself, and closed his eyes quickly. As he stood with his right hand behind him and out of sight, a car flashed across the road. It was doing a hundred if it was moving at all. The patrolman's hat flew off his head and you could already hear the sirens echo across the flatlands.

"God Dammit!!" The patrolman shouted, and he went to retrieve his hat and look down the road. "You!" and he pointed at Sonny here, "You stay here! I'll be back for you!" The man's radio was going crazy with shouting and the man ran to his car and sped off as pebbles exploded like buckshot from the rear tires and his siren screamed in the Texas morning.

Sonny exhaled, once, and watched as another three patrol cars sped after the two lead horses. He closed the trunk, sat in the car, and laughed loudly. Katie looked on in shock.

"Holy shit," he said. "I've been in lots of tight squeezes, darlin, but that one there was about a half second from him losing part of his head. Ha!" he shouted into the ether. "Unbelievable. Shit." He continued saying these expressions as he pulled out onto the road, slowly following the caravan of good guys chasing the bad guys. And the questions therein.

After a mile or so, Katie said, "Weren't we supposed to wait there?"

Sonny glanced at her and looked her face over. "Sweetie," he said, "if we stayed there, we'd be dumber'n him for expecting us to. He made a choice, and it wasn't us. Consider us lucky. Besides, he's one of the lead cars on a chase, now. He's gonna either get the guy or crash, and have about a book's worth of paperwork after. We're nothing but an afterthought for him at this point."

In the distance there rose a plume of black smoke against the desert sky that comes only from machinery. As they approached, they saw three patrol cars lined up and two cars off in the brush. One was another patrol car, probably the lead car, Sonny reasoned, and a 1949 Lincoln Continental Town Sedan, which had flipped once and was now back on its wheels horizontal to the road, looking no less like a bathtub. The officer who had pulled them over was shooting over the roof of his car at the two men crouched behind theirs. The other patrolmen were just now rushing to his aid. As the Merc passed, Sonny slowed at the Lincoln and while he couldn't be positive, Sonny was pretty sure he saw the curlyhaired man from Las Cruces looking at him as he passed. Maybe they *did* need the Merc, he found himself thinking, and it was as honest a thought as he had.

"Y'know, I think I saw that car at our motel," Katie said.

"Really?" Sonny said.

"Y'know, sometimes you're not the most observant guy."

"Huh," Sonny exclaimed, and squinted on the road to El Paso.

***

The Merc passed El Paso and traveled east on roads built for pickups and not for sleds. Sonny and Katie bounced airborne more than once on roads fit for paving. Sonny had no directions, just those borne of a memory and gifted somewhere. They pulled to the ranch gate by mid-afternoon. The sun squatted above the hinterlands like some unblinking eye of the gods of malice.

There was a single word, Del's, across the topmost plank on the fence. Sonny opened the latch on the gate and drove in. It was a driveway that ran for some 200 yards before any structure. Something impractical and from the long ago. They parked and got out and stretched and drew the attention of the three dogs long before anything else. They found Del in the toolshed banging with a hammer, attempting in vain to straighten a piece of sheetmetal beyond hope.

The old man wore a cowboy hat and spectacles and a tshirt that did not fit his protruding belly and a pair of blue jeans. His mustache had grown to unkempt and nearly mythic proportions. "Hot Damn!," he exclaimed upon seeing Sonny and threw his arms around the man twenty-five years his junior.

"Wasn't sure I'd ever see you again, ya outlaw. Hot damn. Well," he said, and shuffled his boots in the dirt. "Lookit yer arms. And neck. And who's this here?"

"Del, this here's Katie. I mighta mentioned her—"

"'Course ya did, Son. I just remember that girl being, well. A girl. *This* her?"

Katie stepped forward with her hand outstretched and the old man took it like a gentleman and kissed it once on the topside, his mustache bristling and tickling her hand at once. "The pleasure's all mine, young lady," he said. "You keeping this man in line? That's no easy task."

"There's no keeping Sonny in line, sir," she said.

"No sir, no sir. I aint your granddaddy. Just call me Del. How about I go inside and get us all some sweet tea and you tell me what in the world you're doin in West Texas?"

Sonny nodded.

The two of them sat on the porch as the sun set low in the west. Sonny had taken the shotgun and walked the perimeter of the place looking for rattlesnakes. Sometimes at night they would encroach upon the house and when morning came Del would wake to a dead dog. Once he awoke to one coiled on the couch that Katie was sitting on (which made Katie stand for a moment and look, as though it were still there). So, each daylight ended with a perimeter search, and Del was happy to pass it off to Sonny once every four years.

"Sorry to hear bout your mom," Del said to Katie.

"Thanks. It's been awhile now. I miss her. But, y'know." She shrugged.

"I lost my wife more than a decade ago. Only woman I was ever with. We dated since high school. Anyways, we dated in Amarillo, Texas, and moved to Austin for college and got married and then to Quantico for the Bureau and then, hell, we were stationed a few places. We moved back here to retire and then she got the cancer."

"I think that's beautiful," Katie said, and nodded as a form of affirmation. "I'm sorry she's gone. She must have been something special."

"Yeah. That she was. She'd have loved to be here, seeing you and Son. But loss is a part of it all."

"It's interesting that you call him that," Katie said. "I've known Sonny since I can remember and he doesn't let anybody call him that."

"What's that, *Son*?"

"Yeah. That."

"Well. I always just figured it short for Sonny. Never much thought about it. But I know that said from the wrong mouth, or in the wrong tone, it can sound awful different."

Sonny walked up the plank steps then and leaned the shotgun against the railing. All clear, he said. Then: "You talking about me up here, old man?"

"Yessir. I am. This young lady says that you don't like bein' called Son. That 'bout right?"

Sonny laughed. "Yeah. Well, if you are gonna call me that, you'd better have earned it. And you did."

"How's that?" Katie asked, leaning forward.

The two men looked at one another.

"You, or me?" Sonny asked Del.

"Take it away, youngster. I'll add as I see fit."

Katie crossed her legs and sank into the moment.

Sonny pulled a wooden chair from the dining room table and flipped it backwards and straddled the thing like a horse.

"Ok. Well, it's 1937 and Del's working Organized Crime and me and H are following Dragna, in LA. The East Coast sends Siegel over to us, and so he and Dragna are working together, running a gambling racket and wiring money back to the East Coast. Easy money, right? Well, we're onto em and these guys here are onto em but we're waiting for a big score, the right timing, because we both know with the lawyers these guys are gonna get, anything less than red-handed means they get off and we get a black mark on the department. Way shit works."

"Anyways," Sonny continued, "so we're following these guys, tapping, stakeouts, all of it, hassling property owners, just good fun, right? Well, one of his Fed guys gets a tip on a huge casino boat off the Santa Monica coast, legit mob run and with the wiring capabilities to boot! All of it at once and it's FBI so we take the lead and he's got his guys and me and H go along and we take a boat out there and it's this huge lighted yacht, five times bigger than any boat you've ever been on, Katie, I mean, this thing just never ends. So, we creep up the sides of the thing like we're all frogmen and we're all a little confused on why it's so quiet. I mean, this is a casino boat, right? Should have people being drunk and rowdy and the whole nine. But it's quiet. And we sneak up to the main ballroom, bust in the side door, yours truly going first like I'm friggin Wyatt Earp and it's a *wedding*! The bride and groom standing up there all dolled up and I'm runnin around with my gun out like a crazy person."

"Not the first time you've been accused of that, neither," interjected Del.

Sonny looked at Del and continued: "Anyways, the tip was way off, but it turns out that this is a big mobster's brother, which is where the tip came from to begin with, and the guy's from Sicily and he thinks we're there for him! So, he takes off out the side and I chase him down and bounce his head off things a coupla times. The rest of the guys stay in the big room to calm people down and make sure the whole thing is legit. So I've got him and I don't even know who the guy is or why he's running, right? And I grab the guy, who's unconscious now, and start dragging him back and outta nowhere, this guy's bodyguard—remember, he was a bigwig back in the homeland—puts iron right behind my ear. And, I mean, I had lost my gun by this point, and I got this Sicilian wop by one arm and I'm dead to rights. And this guy, he's speakin Italian, which doesn't make no sense to me, so I can't even talk to the guy! I'm already thinking of the big ticket—no more Betty, no more baseball games, no more job, nothing, right? And this old guy here, he pointed at Del then, he's got a shotgun on this cat the whole time, standing in the dark. No word, no warning, just a simple blast in the darkness and the bodyguard is splattered all over the night. Musta flew six feet. Never had any idea what hit him. It was fantastic. You—"

"Only man I ever shot, right there. You know that?" Del asked.

Sonny looked at him and said nothing.

"I used to spend some time thinking, too. This guy comes out here, leaves Sicily and his family to watch the guy he's hired to protect, and gets killed doing it. Used to give me nightmares." He shook his head at the thought.

"Well," Sonny said, looking at Katie, "that's why he can call me Son anytime he wants. He earned it. I wouldn't be here if it weren't for him." He looked at Del and nodded, once.

"*This* guy," Del said, pointing towards Sonny, "was unlike anybody I ever saw in the line of fire. No hesitation whatsoever. No blinking. Just like an animal, in a way. And I mean that in a good way, Son. Just...you never doubted him. Like a blunt instrument in a world of angles, I guess."

"Alright. Enough about that," Sonny said, and waved away the suggestion.

"Y'all hungry?" Del asked. "I got some steaks in the fridge."

***

Later, after they had eaten grilled steaks and corn and caught up on Del's history and said goodnight to Katie, the two men sat on the porch in the darkness as the junebugs and mosquitos flew about. Each of them in turn illuminated by lamp. Del broke open the whiskey and started into it. He poured some into a glass for Sonny, who left it on the rail. Once he sniffed it and all sorts of impulses started their engines, but he put it back down and left it there.

"So, whatcha really doin here, Son?" Del asked, with a brace of sobriety.

277

Sonny lit a Chesterfield and exhaled. The he said: "Got a favor to run down in New Orleans. Fully legal. Had a guy die in my arms in LA, Del, and this suitcase is all that's left. Didn't know him, and I don't know who did him. But he asked me with his dying words. Not like I gotta bunch of obligations back home. So I'm going—I mean, what the hell else am I supposed to do, y'know?"

Del looked at Sonny and then at his whiskey and sipped. Then he nodded, once, and said: "K. I'll bite on that. And her?" He nodded towards the house.

"She aint got a mom. She aint got a dad. She's a poker friggin prodigy. She's gotta have somebody. I'm that somebody," he said, and nodded. "'Bout that simple."

"Of all the folks seeking parenthood, I reckon you're not the most suited I can think of. No offense meant," Del said.

"That's harsh, old man." But Sonny nodded after he said it, as much in agreement as anything.

"It is what it is," Del continued. He paused and looked out into the black night. "I mean, you're a wanted man, Sonny. Got things all up and down yer arms and neck and who knows where else. That's not a normal thing for a man to do. And the thing with Betty—"

Sonny looked at him then, hard.

"Look, I don't think now nor did I then that you killed that girl. You were at her beck and call, and saw her as the hand of God. I know it. But you *ran*, Son. You didn't fight it, didn't call on character witnesses like me who could have helped. Didn't clear your name. Just disappeared into thin air like you could fly and then you show up here four years later. And I'll just bet that this trip is like you say it is. But I'll also bet that you had to get out of LA, too. That about right?"

"Big Vin," was all Sonny said in response.

"Mickey's bodyguard? So you go back to LA in some kind of vigilante mission and kill a mob guy. Now where does that leave you? Where does this stop? Look, Son, you've always been one of my favorites, but you've got a girl in there now who's depending on you to steer her on the right path and a life to make somewhere, 'cause you aint getting no younger. How does that happen with the LAPD and the mob looking for you? You tell me," he said, and sat back in his chair, having expressed what was needed. He reached over to the railing and there fingered his corn cob pipe and loaded leaf tobacco into it from a pouch beside it. He lit the thing and pulled on it and the smoke that rose in tufts and smelled of cinnamon.

Sonny sat there for a time saying nothing. Never in his life had he wanted that whiskey perched on the rail more. Never. And had Del not been sitting right there he may very well have taken it. And finished the bottle, after that. Instead, he answered, his voice a strangled fist of rage,

"I'm kind of just taking it a day at a time right now." He paused, as if the words themselves were barbs to swallow. "I got us here. I'll get us to New Orleans."

"Didja talk to your old partner in LA, what was his name? Howard?"

"It's Harold, but yeah. Then he set me up. He must be on Cohen's payroll now. Or just trying to get off the desk duty," Sonny said, and waved a hand at it all, "they tried to hit me once, then killed the girl I was talking to."

"Huh. Well. That's no good atall. I wouldn't have pictured him—are ya sure?"

"Yeah," Sonny said. "Pretty damn sure. Don't see any other way."

"So, then, you aint really got nodody, then, do ya?" He said, as way of a question. "Look, I'll see if can't make a phone call for you."

Sonny looked at him and in that look something needful. Desperate.

"Look, Son. I welcomed you here because you always got a place here. That's the way it is. And you tell that girl in there too. I aint got no family anymore, just poor facsimiles, and you're some of that. So you're always welcome. But you gotta get you straight."

"Yeah. I gotta get New Orleans right. That'll help. I want to thank you. For all of this. You taking us in."

"'Course, Son. You need to leave the girl here while you go handle things?"

Sonny said he'd think about it and went inside. And, laying on his bed, he did think about it until he fell asleep though his reasonings and decisions that night were his and his alone.

A TRUNK FULL OF ZEROES

18.

When he awoke at dawn's first light he was still thinking about it. And as they packed the car, sure to keep quiet, he thought still. He wrote Del a note and left it on the kitchen table and drove off with the Merc chortling heavily in the night air and Katie trying to get back to sleep and he was still thinking about it. He perhaps should have left her there. But he didn't. He couldn't. And that was that. If this is about a man's failures, here was another.

It was about a thousand miles to New Orleans and he planned to take the majority of those miles today. The 90 east had been expanded to four lanes in many areas, and that helped the travel some. Katie slept until near ten, and they were already past Alpine by that point. They stopped to eat breakfast only briefly. Sonny was a driven man now, and would see this thing through to fruition. The afternoon saw them chasing down San Antonio and the newly built Gulf Freeway. This sped things up a bit and they drove through central Texas like he was not a wanted man, not forsaken to gods and man alike. They passed Houston with the uniform decision they would never stop there in the future either, and rolled past. The heat had become palpable and that meant the trip to his birthplace had a reality to it that theory cannot give. The humidity weighed on each of them like an extra layer even with the window open, wind still pooling in the car. It was near dusk when they stopped in Beaumont to get dinner. Two blind turns found them on a street with weeds kneehigh and here were black men of various hue standing around a brickbuilt juke joint with barbecue cooking over hollowed trash cans. Sonny put the .45 into the back of his pants and ordered two plates and returned to the car. They sat, the two of them, in the car and ate as the music bled from the building like something unchained and shouting its name.

"Omigod this is good!" Katie said. "It's like it explodes in your mouth. I just—," and then she stopped talking and dug in again.

Sonny smiled at the discovery and thought back to his childhood. The South can fry anything, and the South can barbecue. They finished their plates and he walked back over and ordered another and gave it to Katie as leftovers upon his return. He stretched briefly outside the car and saw nightfall on the horizon.

Within the hour darkness had settled and thereafter they crossed the state line into Louisiana. Texas carries with it a history peculiar unto itself with Rangers and oil and cowboys but Louisiana recalls another planet entire. Cajun and Black and Southern cultures stewed together but never quite one. All enmeshed amid the blues and the unforgiving humidity, forced to become something other altogether. Sonny figured they would reach New Orleans by around ten o' clock.

They passed Lake Charles and the willows hung above the road nearly close enough to touch. They gassed up in Lafayette to drive the bayou south and passed by New Iberia and Morgan City and soon were in Houma. Katie had fallen asleep out of sheer boredom and Sonny searched the radio dial. He found a disc jockey who called himself Dr. Daddy-O and set the dial there. He introduced *Jungle Blues* by Fats Domino as Sonny drove northeast into New Orleans, the city an illuminated pearl against the opalescent darkness of the Mississippi and its shores.

***

Sonny crossed the narrow Huey P. Long Bridge and continued east on the 90 towards the heart of the city. As he neared the French Quarter, the din of activity began to pronounce itself. Every night in the quarter was a party; the size of the party depended on circumstance. He turned left on Decatur and the activity was palpable. He wanted to wake Katie and show her but knew that once woke, she wouldn't be going down anytime soon. And that didn't help anyone. Besides, he planned on staying here for a couple of nights. New Orleans was no place to visit for a day. Tomorrow they would take in the Quarter, the French Market, and the like. Walk the streets. The next day they would deliver the bag to Hank's wife and kid. That's how it would go. After that, well. Sonny threw that thought away. After that would take care of itself.

One day at a time, he thought, as he passed Jackson Square and saw a HOTEL sign immediately after, hanging from a scrolled colonnade and the bougainvillea that draped from it. He made a left on St. Ann and parked the car behind a pickup filled with crates of vegetables. He locked the car with Katie in it and walked into the hotel.

The lobby was whitewalled and well-lighted, with gold candelabras over a maroon carpet split with a fleur-de-lis design and a man in a suit behind the counter. The stairs were immediately behind the desk, spinning ornately upward. The desk itself was marble. It looked like a radio televangelist's vision of heaven, and Sonny felt like the first customer ever.

"Hello there, sir," the man said, neither smarmy or sarcastic, with barely a hint of accent.

"Hey. I need a room. Two nights. Two beds."

"Do you have a reservation with us?" He asked.

"No. But I have money to pay like I don't need one," Sonny said.

"I see," the man said. "Are you on vacation?"

Sonny laughed at that. "Is anybody here not? Why would you get a hotel room in the French Quarter at these prices if you were a resident?" He asked the questions, but his usual level of disdain was markedly reduced. The kid seemed decent, and Sonny had just driven for seventeen hours. He just wanted a room. Any room.

"I've got two available, though only one with two beds."

"I'll take it."

"Okay," the kid said. He was tan and his teeth white and the world was an oyster unshucked and his alone. Sonny wanted to tell him that the oyster held no pearl. That in fact the oyster itself was boobytrapped and put there only for your fingerprints. That happiness was like catching a snowflake. Once you get it, it doesn't exist anymore. he thought all of these things, and said none of them. Then the kid said, "And how will you be paying for this?"

"I got cash, kid. And gimme the papers to fill out, I'll take em to my room. You'll get em tomorrow. I been driving for damn near a day and I just want to sleep." The truth, he thought—how nice to simply convey the truth.

The man looked at Sonny without expression. Then finally he said: "Okay. Just be sure and turn them in tomorrow. I'll leave a note with the morning manager." He handed Sonny the key and an envelope. Sonny paid, and slipped the kid a tip.

He unpacked the car, first Katie and then the bags, before sitting himself on the bed. The room was on the 2nd floor with brick walls and black ironwork bedframes. There was a deck as well, but he wasn't going out there tonight. He slid Hank's bag under his bed, put the other in the space between his bed and Katie's and fell asleep almost immediately, his right hand loosely about the grip of his gun.

He awoke to Katie singing badly in the shower and morning light through the sliding glass door. He thought the garbled wobble was the Hank Williams song that he heard, but it could have been jazz improvisation with the way it sounded. It's a good thing she's got poker talent, he found himself thinking.

He picked up the phone and called the lobby for coffee. By the time it had arrived, he already had the paperwork completed to a Mr. William Graves from Mexico (he didn't know why he hadn't used that before, now that he thought about it) and his clothes set out on his bed. The coffee that arrived was an Au Lait and he drank it down while he smoked a Chesterfield on the deck. It was ironwrought and reeked of an old world he enjoyed but knew no part of. The patio area below had tables for dining and a fountain.

Katie peeked her head out onto the deck, hair still wet. She hugged Sonny once and said, "Good morning." Then she peeked into the courtyard and disappeared. There were clouds yet in the distance,

thunderheads even, bringing something else to the day. But they were in

New Orleans, no longer running, and here for something good. Sonny

finished the last of the Au Lait and went in to ready himself.

After showering and dressing he felt like a real person again. Something of

worth. He wore a checked collared shirt over a wifebeater and a pair of

chinos and his brogues. He looked at his snapcap but decided instead on

the fedora and filled his pocket with a wad of cash. Katie was dressed in a

navy polkadot dress and white flats. Sonny saw her and thought she

looked fantastic, but then thought of the worry it would provide him

throughout the day. Then he quickly moved on to the thought of how a

boy would have been easier.

They walked down the stairs and out the lobby and onto St. Ann.

It was a spring morning in the South when the humidity had not yet kicked

in though it would shortly while the clouds covered the brightness of the

sun. The travelers picked their direction blindly and chose right first and

footed their way across Chartres and Royal to Bourbon St, and walked it

down. There were street vendors looking for attention and a group of

three young men playing trumpets for change collected into an upturned

derby hat. They walked into art galleries and clothing shops and even a

boot shop for Sonny, who had heard of the custom alligator boots and wanted a look. They bought only a polka dot scarf for Katie but the morning was filled with something pure and unfamiliar. Sonny was able to smile without malice but in joy, and Katie could simply be a kid.

Along Decatur they walked the French Market and there bought lunch and finished with a plate of beignets and Au Lait at Café Du Monde. Afterwards they walked Jackson Square, pigeons flapping in mockflight as they passed. They took in Jackson's equestrian statue and the magnificent oaks that columned it. From there they crossed St. Peter and took in a Dixieland jazz show and walked the boulevard and ate the city whole. They finished over a plate of jambalaya and red beans and rice so large that the two of them failed to clean it. Sonny had so badly wanted Katie to feel a sense of the city, and he felt that she had. For a day, just one, he felt a deserved father figure. He had given her something she would recall at any point in the modicum of a life, and there was a pride in that. They walked back to the hotel, and she was alight with the day. She was young and gorgeous, and the whole city knew it, while Sonny felt happy but hollow, and couldn't finger why. There was no particular reason he could ascertain, but that did nothing to take from him the certainty of it.

In their room upstairs she changed into pajamas and flopped onto the bed. She told him that she was determined to finish the Thompson novel tonight. Sonny looked himself in the mirror and nodded in confirmation of his hearing, but little else. He had come so far and had arrived nowhere, he thought. He replaced the fedora with his snapcap, turned and said, "Hey, I'm gonna go downstairs, hit a bar, I think. Get some coffee. I had a great time with you today, but I want to give you your own time. You deserve it." He felt filthy for lying to her. When he had said it before, he had meant it. But this time it was for him.

She feigned concern for a moment and then agreed willingly. She had her book to read, after all, and a deck on which to read it, and the majesty of a city just beyond. He kissed the top of her head and walked out the door and down the stairs mad enough to kill somebody, and he had no idea what for.

19.

There is truth in men's lives, and then there is that thing unexplainable that resides deeper than truth that they have no words for. Sonny exited the hotel and immediately walked across St. Ann to the lighted church on Chartres. He walked the steps and topmost the old wooden doors splayed open like any desire, anywhere. Inside, there were candles aflame and Jesus pendant and women sitting quietly in the wooden pews—some of them held candles as well. He alone the sole male violating something so silent and without name. He sat in the rearmost pew and made the sign of the cross for Betty. For Miryea, and her misfortune of meeting him. For Katie, the hopes for her therein. He stood then and lighted a Chesterfield and walked out of the place. He would not bother with himself. Those undeserving even without bounds of hypocrisy.

He walked St. Ann north looking for a bar. He had lied to Katie earlier, and felt a heel for it. But New Orleans seemed an end writ and therein bags for widows and safety for Katie but he would have none of it.

He felt electric, jolted through with a malice undeserving of the time or place. He turned right on Bourbon St and there an establishment, narrow and deep, with an old marble counter and a tinmetal Dixie Beer sign over the mirror behind the bar. The tiles on the floor were black and white, tiny octagons forming stars given perspective. He did not see the name of the joint, and it did not matter. It was merely context. He sidled to a table and leaned against the back pew opposite the bar. There were two men on stools, singly, and a group of four boys in the back of the place. College kids, it looked and sounded like. The barkeep nodded his way.

"What'll it be?"

"A Jax and a double Beam, neat," Sonny said. He rolled up his sleeves in the warm night and lighted a smoke and blew at the ceiling.

The barkeep brought them and they sat on the table for a time. The Beam gleaned a caramel radiance, all stillwater in spirit. The Jax bubbled like it were a living thing entire, the glass frosted over in cold. He stared at them. It was like an imaginary conversation. He did not want to listen to them, these omens. But they were his own now, his madness and burden. And still, he neglected them. He watched the bartender watch him not drinking them. He watched both of the men at the bar leave. The ashtray was fourdeep in soldiers when finally, without explanation or motive, he shot back the bourbon and sipped deeply the cold beer. He wiped his watering eye upon finishing. There were failures in life, and

Sonny had a skill for making his spectacular. He ordered another round and then another. The night began to slow a bit and the bar leaned. The boys in back were drunk now, drunker than he, and were making a racket something wild. One of them was dryhumping the table, obviously a visual aid in a story, and the rest of them laughing. Two of them walked to the bar for replenishment.

"What you boys know about fuckin?" Sonny asked.

One of the boys turned and looked at him, then turned away. He hit his friend on the arm and said something and then other boy looked back at Sonny's arms. It was like they were the paying customers, and he was the lion at the zoo. Except there were no iron bars, here.

"I said, what you boys know about fuckin?"

The first boy, with curly blonde hair and a red sweater on, turned and said: "We don't know nothing, mister. Just havin some fun is all."

"You boys wouldn't know how to have fun if you were bucknaked in a Spanish Fly whorehouse. Shit," he exclaimed. Then he motioned to the bartender, who had begun to weary of him already, and said, "One more round, right here, please."

The bartender feigned defiance as he readied the order.

The second boy, larger by a quarter than the first and wearing a varsity football sweater, said something to the curly haired boy, who shushed him.

The drinks were delivered and Sonny shot back the Beam before it even had the opportunity to still.

The boys were obviously having a discourse on cojones while their brethren in back pounded the table in laughter. "Fuck that," the second boy said to the first, mostly under his breath.

"It appears you two boys been having a lover's quarrel, that 'bout right?" Sonny said, loud enough to carry to the back table. His Southern accent had returned with the bourbon. A part of him, somewhere buried at the moment, thought: interesting.

"Least I aint some drunk all painted up like a *freakshow*," the second boy turned and spat. He paused, and then finished with: "Nice black eye."

There were many things at that particular point in time that could have been said, but that was not the best.

Sonny smiled at the boy, and said: "Ah, look. The varsity boy's got a set. Well, sweetcakes, this here is my first real drink in nearly four years. I will now give you the opportunity to take back those things you just said about me, or I will break shit on you that you did not know could be broken. I give you that choice." He raised his beer in toast, and sipped.

"Fuck you," the boy in the football sweater said, and he faced Sonny, leaning with his elbows on the bar behind him.

"Whoo!" Sonny hooted, and brought his pint glass up in salute. "That is fantastic. You are so green you don't have your mama's sense, do ya, boy? There's pride, and there's just bein a dumbass, son, and you don't know the difference."

"Least I aint a tattooed freak, cryin all the time," the boy said, referring to the teardrop on Sonny's cheek.

Sonny threw the pint glass then at the boy's face, hitting him in the mouth. The boy immediately bent double and Sonny was on him in two steps and brought his knee to the young man's face, twice. He fell to the ground and curled into the fetal position, his mouth and nose not resembling the mouth and nose from just moments ago. A crimson pool began to spread like a two-dimensional halo across the black and white tiled floor. One of his friends was shouting something but making no move to help and the other two in the back were drunk enough to just now realize what was happening.

The bartender, however, had pulled the shotgun from beneath the bar and its double bores rested not two feet from where Sonny stood.

"Git up," Sonny yelled at the boy. "Git up!"

"That's enough of that, mister," the barkeep said. "I'll shoot ya full of buckshot if you don't—"

In one motion, Sonny leaned onto the bar as if to take a shot from his empty Beam and grabbed the barrel of the shotgun and wrenched it from the man's hands before he could finish his threat. "You aint doin

shit," Sonny said, and turned the barrel onto the boy on the ground. "Git

the fuck up, boy!" he shouted.

He pressed the barrel against the ear of the boy in the varsity

sweater and said: "I'mma ask you one more time."

His friends were all shouting, "Get up, Ryan!" in different cadence

and rhythm but the affect was the same.

The kid in the sweater looked up at Sonny, his nose a mess of

blood and his mouth missing two teeth and those intact stained across, and

he got to his knees. "Now look here," Sonny said. "What you did was

damn stupid. You don't call on a man my size who looks like me for fun.

This what happens, right here. But you got more guts in you than every

one a your pussy-ass friends combined." He brought the shotgun barrel up

at his friends as if pointing at them, and said, "You can't hold a fuckin

candle to your boy Ryan here. Each one a you go home and sleep on that.

Fuckin sissy boys, every one of you." He spat on the floor as he finished.

"You're still a fucker," Ryan managed to blurt, blood running

down his chin as he spoke, the f in his expletive reduced to a lisp on account

of his missing teeth.

Sonny smiled then. "Yeah, yeah. I am. You got me there," he

said, and chuckled at the thought. Then he reached out with his free hand

he wiped the boy's chin free of blood. Nobody knew why then and they still don't. He pumped the shotgun twice with the hand that held it and removed the shells, placing the empty weapon on the marble. Then he turned to the barkeep and said: "I'll take that bottle of Beam." He wrapped the bloody hand around the neck of the bottle and dropped a hundred dollar bill in its place.

"You see that that boy gets whatever he wants to drink and some care for that mouth, now," Sonny said, and put another hundred in the young man's hand. Then he walked out. Nobody said anything. They all just stood there, as most people do.

He walked St. Ann's in the darkness down to the hotel sipping from the bottle. He could feel the boy's blood drying on his hand. He reached the hotel and stared at it and instead walked across the street to Jackson Square. There was a scrolled iron bench apart from the statue of Andrew Jackson and Sonny sat there and lighted a cigarette and drank the Beam directly. Minutes later a car of New Orleans finest passed quickly with their sirens on and Sonny sat and watched them. Then another. He'd need to cover his arms and keep a watchful eye tomorrow, he knew that now. He looked at the statue and the man atop the horse who was an American lion and no friend to the Indian and exhaled. History celebrated victory, no doubt about that, Sonny thought. He drank deeply to the thought. The bourbon had gone to a place of warmth that he had long forgotten. He missed the drink terribly, but knew now that he could not visit often. Like the memory of his wife, each visit carried with it some small death in himself.

When he had finished the bottle, he staggered across the street to the hotel and made an Olympic event of the stairs and opened the door to his room with his key after several inaccurate attempts. Katie sat up in bed with the nightstand light on and brought her hand to her mouth upon his entering. He fell at once onto his bed and rolled there. Katie saw the blood on his hand and blood on the knee of his pants and said: "Omigod are you *okay?*," and she rushed to his side and smelled the liquor on his breath and there passed a look undecipherable though no less sympathetic.

"I had some whiskey. First in a long time," he told her. After a pause: "I'm not proud of it."

She put her hands into his and said: "It's okay, Sonny. We all need a little help sometimes." She had started crying but tried not to show it and wiped a tear with her shoulder.

"Don't cry, sweetie," he stammered. "I gotta tell you something. I aint never told anybody," he said breathlessly. "Nobody."

He rolled off the bed and sat with his legs straight and his back against the side of the mattress. His hat had fallen off and his hair askew. He looked every bit of 42 and dissembled. She sat on the floor next to him and held his hand caked in the boy's blood. "Okay," she said. "Go ahead."

"I *shot* Betty," he said in a slurred whisper, simply. "I didn't mean to. I walked in on her and the guy, and my gun was already up because I heard noises, and," he was slurring badly and he sniffed here, collecting what was left of decorum, "they were naked in the bedroom and I"— Sonny stopped and stared straight ahead. She held his hand and looked at him, wordlessly. Completely bereft of a handle of thought. Nobody said anything for a time. Then: "I meant to shoot *him*," he said in a throaty whisper. "She said 'no, Sonny', and moved in front the guy. My name," he slurred, "my name was the last thing she said. I shot her twice. She was the only girl I ever loved and I shot her twice. He said it as though he couldn't believe it either. I shot her, Katie. I didn't mean to. I swear to God I didn't mean to," he said, and broke into sobs that were more bestial than anything Katie had ever heard. She held him there as his body shook and she whispered *shhhh* and brought the blanket from the bed and lay with him through the night.

20.

The following morning the sun rose as normal and the South carried with it a heat as though the devil himself had brought a match to the skin of the world. Katie rose and showered and dressed herself and ordered coffee for Sonny and tipped the waiter when he arrived.

Sonny, for his part, sat up and accepted the coffee. His head felt three sizes too small and the hangover he had was not the worst of it. With some effort, he walked to the balcony and stood there in the sunlight squinting with his Au Lait that he held in the hand stained with another man's blood. He would never tell anybody again what he said last night, and wondered at the ramifications of such a declaration. He would never hurt Katie, never, so she was free to do with it as she would. He thought about this as the sun felt downright mean on his skin.

He came inside when he had finished and she sat on her bed reading. It was a new book. Something by Chandler that he hadn't seen before. She saw him looking at it and said, "This is the new one, *The Little*

Sister." I'll give it to you when I'm done. She smiled at him and that was the whole of it.

He went into the shower and wondered where she had gotten the book without him noticing. He wondered why he had ordered drinks last night rather than coffee. But mostly, he spent the time trying desperately to feel human again. He shaved his two-day beard in the steam of the bathroom when he got out and dressed in a checked shirt and flatfront chino's and walked into the bedroom. He sat on the bed putting on his socks and brogues when suddenly Katie said, "Thanks for telling me last night. I won't ever tell anybody, Sonny. I know you didn't mean to." She started to say more, and stopped herself.

He nodded, once. And that was it. He continued putting on his shoes and then his snapcap and when they were both ready for the day, he said: "Thanks, sweetheart. I truly, truly mean that. Now, let's don't ever mention it again." He exhaled. "So, are we ready for this?" And he motioned to Hank's bag on the bed.

"I think so," she said. "You're gonna do most of the talking, right?"

"I think I have to," he said, as much to himself as to her.

***

They took a taxi to the address on the letter he held and stood outside the single bungalow home. It had a small chainlink fence around the outside and three steps that led to the front door. Sonny felt somehow that he was returning home in some way as well. This was not his family, not in any way, but felt some responsibility nonetheless. He wore it like a heavy crown, and felt as much as he climbed the stairs. Katie followed behind him.

He knocked at the front door three times.

Nobody answered, and he had begun to turn back to Katie when the door opened a third and a pretty mulatto woman appeared. Her voice was friendly but her eyes guarded as she said, "May I help you?"

Sonny looked at her and said, "I've got something of your late husband's, Etta."

She opened the door and invited them in. Theo was playing ball in the back yard and she called him in as well. They sat on the couch and Etta and Theo sat in opposite chairs in the small living room as they faced each other.

"First off, Ma'am. I'm very sorry to bear this. I didn't ask for it," Sonny said.

Etta carried with her a demeanor set stronger than Sonny had expected. She sat and bore the words with grace. And then added, "Somebody called us two days ago. Said that Hank's body had been identified in Los Angeles. It's very difficult, you must imagine," she went on, "to wait for your husband's arrival after his release from prison, to hear such a thing." She paused, collecting the moment by sheer will. "It's taken quite a toll on Theo and I." Her mouth quivered when she spoke, and she held her son's hand in the telling.

"He died with me, ma'am," Sonny said. "I don't know why he was there, and I didn't ask. All I know is I found him in a state and he asked me, as he was dying, to get this bag to you. He told me to tell you how much he loved you, and Theo"—Sonny looked at the boy—"he told me to tell you how proud he was of you. All I can tell you, ma'am, is that it was clear that he wanted very, very badly to just *be here*. And I can see why."

Etta's eyes watered but her etiquette was such that she would not have admitted it. Theo did not bear that burden and had tears running down his cheeks and stood to hug his mother.

"I went back to his motel after he was gone and retrieved this bag," Sonny said, and handed to her.

She wept openly now, finally, and took the bag and told her son, as if Sonny and Katie were not there at all, how when she emptied this bag it was his forever and to take care of his daddy's bag. She zipped it open and then held up the shrinkwrapped cash with wide eyes and took out Hank's belongings, and then the letters and pictures, placing them on the living room table as if the care showed them could manifest itself as something larger than memory.

"I, umm, looked at some of the letters," Sonny admitted. "I apologize. But I wouldn't have found you without them. And the pictures, well, they helped."

He didn't explain why and didn't need to.

Upon leaving, Theo had gone inside, and Sonny stood on the porch before making his way down. Etta placed her hand on Sonny's and said, "I can't imagine why you came all the way from California just to drop off my husband's bag in person. But know that Theo and I will remember this day forever, this unexpected act of kindness, and remember what a good and decent man you must be." She slapped the top of his hand twice softly to bring home her point, and bit her lip to keep from crying.

"It was my pleasure, ma'am," he said. And it was.

***

Sonny and Katie took a cab back to the quarter and loaded their bags in the trunk of the Merc. It was still damn hot but there was a storm brewing somewhere off the coast and the echo of the thunder could be heard even now. They walked a bit of the quarter, and Sonny bought a pair of cowboy boots at the specialty shop, they wore a dark brown patina and rounded toes in the buckaroo style, simply because he had always wanted cowboy boots and never bought any. Now, they would remind him of New Orleans and this trip, of its failures and possible vindication. Then towards St. Ann south to Decatur and sat outside under the green and white striped awning at Café Du Monde.

They had eaten a plate of powdered beignets and sucked down their Au Lait's when Katie said, "I *gotta* get in a game, Sonny. It's been, like, I don't know? What, a week, maybe?"

Sonny smiled at the admission. "Yeah, well, I was thinking," he said.

"Thinking what?" she asked.

"Thinking I might know someplace perfect where I could hire out certain services and you could continue to learn your craft," he answered.

"No!," she said. And she pounded the table with both palms and leaned forward, her eyes unblinking.

Sonny said nothing, lit a cigarette for affect.

"You mean it?" she said. "We can go *there*?" She was getting frantic now.

"I got some friends there that owe me favors. Might be able to get me a license, whatever the name. And you? You'll get to play the best, little girl."

"VEGAS? Really?"

"Vegas, darlin," Sonny answered, and exhaled onto Decatur as the small rain from a large storm began to tiptoe about the quarter.

About the Author:

Brian Townsley is the author of three books of poetry, as well as the Sonny Haynes books *A Trunk Full of Zeroes* and *Outlaw Ballads*. He has won national awards for his writing, as well as had short stories and poems published in everything from *Berkeley Poetry Review* to *Frontier Tales*, from *Black Mask* and *Mystery Tribune* to *Killpoet* and *Quarterly West*, among many others. He also had a Sonny Haynes story make the Distinguished List in *Best American Mystery Stories, 2019*. He is a podcaster and executive editor for Starlite Pulp, as well as an alum of the mighty California Golden Bears and USC Trojans, and lives in Southern California.

A TRUNK FULL OF ZEROES

313

www.ingramcontent.com/pod-product-compliance
Lightning Source LLC
Chambersburg PA
CBHW071303140726
47996CB00005B/1611